Everything's Cool

Justin Carroll

Copyright © 2012 Justin Carroll

All rights reserved.

Cover art and design by Nathanael Rouillard

ISBN-13: 978-1481261883

ACKNOWLEDGMENTS

Huge thanks to Jojo Thomas for her insight and support, and to the gang - Robin Bayley, Al Anderson, Caroline Swain, Alex Foley and Jennie Pittam.

Justin Carroll

CHAPTER 0
FRIDAY

The strip-light hums, a convergence of sound and light just above his head. He breathes deeply, lungfuls of bleach and urine. Lets the hum fill his ears, drowning out his thoughts as the not-bright-enough neon tube flickers, light in its death throes.

His hands shake as he clutches the small vial. He pierces the foil, slides the needle inside, and pulls gently. Withdraws the point, squeezes. A tear glides along the smooth, unblemished metal.

He's nervous, excited. He hasn't done this before, but he's studied Trainspotting and Pulp Fiction. He doesn't have a belt. He uses the Saran Wrap, twisted into a tight, plastic cord. He rests the syringe on a metallic paper dispenser defaced by blue pen: *Frankie Fucked Here*. He wraps the Saran Wrap around and around. He should have studied knots.

Stan steadies himself. He needs to get this right first time or he'll lose his nerve. His thumb caresses the skin below the Saran Wrap until he sees purple snaking, pulsing. The beating wars with the stuttering of the strip-light. He blinks, closes his eyes, focuses. Places the needle and applies pressure. It slips through skin and he feels the slightest resistance as he enters the vein. He pauses, remembering the image of blood swirling in fluid. He pushes, slowly, gently.

Her honey-colored eyes widen. She whines through the gag.

"I'm sorry. But, I have to know what you know. I need to stop it." He'd tell her if he thought she'd believe him. But she wouldn't, so he swallows the words and hopes his eyes convey apology. He has no choice.

The hum continues, keeping them safe as he lets the Sodium Pentothal take effect.

CHAPTER 1
TUESDAY

He knows how it will end. How it will start. Chaos and riots. War and blood. He's known it for as long as he's known he was breathing. It's always there, the burden of truth, the weight of knowledge. Ignorance *is* bliss. He longs for bliss, to walk and talk, to work and fight and fuck without thought for the future.

He turns his Walkman up as he walks. The tape inside continues to play the comforting sound of white noise – the transitory fizz of the radio. He lets it fill him, suffuse him. While it plays, he's safe. They can't find out that he knows, which means they've no reason to find him. He looks up instinctively. Between the skyscrapers the sky, so blue it makes his eyes ache, is empty.

He'd be safer inside. He speeds up, eyes fixed on the concrete beneath him, taking in the scars it bears: the grey-black stains of cast-off chewing gum, the cracks and chips from a thousand-thousand feet. He weaves above it, avoiding suits and coats, careful not to touch anyone. He doesn't want to be infected by anything. He doesn't want anyone to be able to follow him either, to drop something in a pocket or stick something to him.

He works about a thirty-minute walk from his apartment. The walk takes him an hour each way. He wanders in a big square, varying the route. Got to shift the routine, always one step ahead.

Rush hour swirls around him, people and cars spewed on to the streets, leading their tiny lives. Ignorant, pointless victims or complicit traitors to their own race. He sneers at them, but makes sure no one can see him. He doesn't want to get beaten up or stabbed. There is too much to do and too little time, he tells himself. Justified cowardice.

No one greets him as he shuffles through the revolving door. Concrete becomes wiry mat becomes scuffed marble. He hates the marble, a grandiose testament to a company's wealth and importance, so shortsighted and self-obsessed.

He walks across the foyer, looking left and right. Nothing's changed. He relaxes a little as he passes through the glass door and into the sprawling, painfully organized 'open-plan' office. L-shaped desks placed just so, in accordance with some new-age take on age-old philosophies, each one cordoned off by low, temporary walls. He smiles to himself. They still haven't realized each little cubicle forms one arm of a swastika. He shakes his head, but avoids meeting anyone's gaze as he makes his way along the narrow walkways.

He settles at his arm of the Third Reich and turns on the monitor. The fat, squat box whirrs as it warms up. Before the black screen fades into harsh white and brand compliant yellow, he stares at his own distortion. He should probably shave, but he's been too busy.

He's replaced by figures and numbers, requests to fix this issue and that 'technical problem'. Reluctantly, he turns off his Walkman. He's not safe in the office, but it's a risk he has to take.

People pass by him. Most ignore him, some don't.

"Stan? Stan! I thought you'd fix my mouse thing today? I can't get the little arrow to move." He nods, mutters "Ignorant ape."

"What?" The blue suit with the smug face and perfect hair leans over the little wall.

"Absolutely. I'll get to it as soon as I can, Geoff." He attempts a smile. He knows it looks ridiculous.

More exchanges like this. He visits various desks, presses on/off switches, pushes cables back into boxes. Fixes problems that a child of five could solve. He wonders, not for the first time, why he is bothering. These people aren't worth saving.

Hours tick by.

He eats lunch at his desk. No meat, no unknown chemicals or mind-altering substances. Bread from a local bakery he knows hasn't been compromised, and a particular brand of plastic cheese squares that he has investigated thoroughly and knows, beyond any doubt, is safe. While he eats he turns off his monitor and takes the phone off the hook. When he's finished he folds the sandwich bag away.

"Hey, Stan."

He looks up. It's some ignorant from upstairs. Kevin, Colin? "Hi."

Whoever-he-is smiles convincingly and Stan almost

believes it. "Hey there. I just wanted to introduce you to a new starter we've got upstairs. She's working in Internal Affairs, so she's probably going to come to you with reporting requests." Whoever-he-is ushers her forward.

Stan stands up and forces his eyes to meet hers. She clearly pretends to ignore the crumbs that tumble to the floor, tiny indictments screaming at her that she shouldn't even touch him. He doesn't hold out his hand. There's no point.

"Hello there, Stan. I'm Rachel. Pleased tameetcha." She runs the words together in an overly-familiar way. She curvy, bigger than that slim ideal. Plain-faced. But, her eyes are beautiful. Her blonde hair, for some reason he can't explain, is alluring. He feels his cheeks warming, all the more because he's aware of it. Then Rachel smiles, and he feels the warmth drain from him. It's a knowing smile, a conspiratorial smile. A traitorous smile.

He swallows hard. Attempts his ridiculous grin again while nodding and fumbling some sort of greeting. "Very nice to, um, how do you... yes."

Whoever-he-is chuckles. "We should probably be carrying on. Lots more people to meet."

Rachel nods, and smiles again at Stan, fixing him with her eyes. "It was great tameetcha."

Stan nods.

The two of them walk off, and he hears Whoever-he-is telling her "He's weird, but he's great to have around, a real whizz with computers."

He slumps into his chair. His heart is racing. He feels a thin bead of sweat sliding down his side from his armpit.

The rest of the day passes in agonizing slow-motion. He

keeps his head down, avoids going upstairs in case Rachel sees him, can study him or follow him. He has to get home. He has to work out how she found him, how they found him. He might have to change jobs, even move again.

At 5pm exactly, he grabs his bag, turns off his monitor and shuffles out of the office as quickly as he can without drawing attention. He takes an hour and a half to get home.

CHAPTER 2
TUESDAY, WEDNESDAY

He arrives home and turns on his stereo. White noise floods the room, polystyrene packing chips of sound hiding him from the outside world.

His small apartment has only one internal wall, dividing the living area from the bathroom. The bed is in one corner, the desk by the only window. A small kitchen, pristine, against the wall furthest from the bed. A leather armchair and a small television and VHS video player (unplugged), that came with the flat, in the middle of the room. And boxes. Dozens of boxes. Shoeboxes, moving boxes, discarded cereal boxes. His research, his library and records. A testament to his focus on saving the world.

He prepares a meal of organically grown vegetables, bought from a small store owned by an elderly man who believes the Russians won the Cold War and are secretly running the country. He can be trusted. Stan roasts the vegetables with some natural oil from the same store. Boils some rice. Mixes them together and eats some nuts for protein. Everything is sourced carefully, from reputable companies with no ties to the government.

He turns on his computer and, after a while, he's connected. He spends the night on the World Wide Web, searching through databases for a clue, trying to find anything that would indicate they'd found him.

He's cracked a few sites that the government uses to transfer research data. He's been following their progress. He needs to know how much time he has. Nothing that he can find leads him to her. Nothing whispers they've caught him. It is a worrying coincidence.

He gives up on Rachel. He'll have to find another way to work out how she found him, what she knows. For now, he'll settle for continuing to uncover the investors behind the two companies he is certain will be responsible.

He's printed off financial reports, sought out newspaper clippings, and looked through the microfiches at libraries. There is nothing that he does not know about them.

They were founded in the 70's, both are in America and HQ'd in the city. Delphic Electronics and The Tiresias Corporation. Their C.E.O's are both influential, innovative and powerful. They have been developing competing software and hardware for over twenty years.

They are both fronts for the government, performing secret research into developing something that will end the world.

Project Cassandra.

He doesn't know what it is, what it does. He only knows the name. And they know he knows. Or they know someone knows. And they block his attempts at uncovering more. He's a mouse, but he never thought that the cat would catch him so quickly. He needs more time. He needs to know what they are doing so he can find out how to stop them.

His eyes hurt. Pain in his head flares with each heartbeat. He closes down his internet browser window and turns off his computer. He's reviewed the maps of the buildings a dozen times, they don't reveal anything. He can't think straight, not now. He needs to sleep.

He moves to his bed. It's small, old. The sort of bed found in prisons or scout huts. The thick, wavy springs that the thin mattress rests on squeal and whine as he sits. He removes his boots, his trousers. Unbuttons his shirt and tosses it in the wash basket. The trousers he folds and places on the floor. He lies down, pulls the rough woolen blanket up to his chin. Sleeps.

Chaos. People flowing like a screaming, bleeding sea between buildings that topple and crumble into themselves. He stands on high, looking down at the tatters of humanity. Blood and fear and shit mingle in his nostrils. He watches.

The surging tide disappears into smoke. The world struggles to draw breath as it dies beneath his feet.

He can see them. Weapons and machines. The blood. He can smell them, under the sanguine copper, the unwholesome cleanliness of hospitals and laboratories.

But he can't hear them, can't hear anything over the fizz of white noise. It hides him and he stands, invisible and omniscient.

He holds something in his hands. A sphere. Uneven and warm. He feels death getting closer. He sees the pathetic victims of their own ignorance cowering in corners, in dead-end streets, waiting for the end.

He stands and raises the globe above his head. He shouts, but his words are lost in static. The smoke stops, the screech of machines fades. He alone stands as guardian to his race.

He looks up. The globe drips with dark, coagulated blood. Its eyes are wide, staring into the distance. He does not recognize the face, but he knows it. It is the face of the man who will start the end of everything.

The smoke clears and all about him are men and women and children. They sob with joy, kneel before him and beg him to touch them. He is their savior. They love him. They need him.

Awake. He lies there, sweating and panting. The power, the love and adoration, has left him weak and aroused.

He has not dreamt of a face before. He gropes for his pad and pencil. Sketches what he remembers. Vague recollections. A familiar mystery.

Early morning insomnia. He waits, only half-hoping sleep will reclaim him. It doesn't. He is ready for his alarm clock at six-thirty, preemptively stopping the tiny hammer.

Trousers, clean shirt, clean socks. No breakfast. His stomach twists inside him as he thinks about Rachel. The spy.

She poses questions he cannot answer. How did she find him? Who sent her? What does she know, or what does she suspect?

He makes his lunch quickly, in a perverse rush to reach work to encounter the woman he desperately wants to avoid.

He slips the Walkman into his pocket and slides the headphones over his short hair. Presses 'play', and simultaneously turns off the stereo. Picks up his keys and bag, leaves the apartment and locks the three metal locks.

The sky is that unreal blue. No clouds to offer a sense of depth or reality. He walks quickly, feeling his armpits growing damp. He takes only forty-five minutes to reach work; the pressing need to get close to the mole driving him through the shoals of people as they swarm along roads, huddle at crossings, and then swarm again. He is careful to avoid eye contact, careful to avoid touching anyone. Tempers the urgency with simple common sense: don't get caught.

Concrete, mat, marble. Through the doors and to his swastika arm. Checks he has nothing urgent to deal with. Three 'too stupid to turn on a box', two 'a cable's fallen out and too stupid to realize' and one 'I'd really like your assistance with running a report, could you come upstairs and find me when you're in'.

Rachel.

He feels the heat pushing through his skin, forced out by the cold fear inside him. Yes, the government has resources he doesn't, and yes if they've been watching him for some time then this was almost routine. But it isn't possible. He's too careful.

The fear won't leave him, coils around his intestines. He's lost in a maze of his own devising. Every path leads to a dead-end. He can't avoid her, can't confront her.

He emails her. Short, brief. No chance of profiling.

```
Rachel
I can help this afternoon - 2.45pm.
Stan
```

Lunch. He takes his phone off the hook, but can't eat. He

stares at the pockets of air in the bread, at the soft ridges of the crust.

He puts on his headphones and presses play. Closes his eyes. Thinks. He knows he's being investigated because she's here. She knows about him, because she's here and she's making up excuses to spend time with him. He needs to know what she knows, and find out who sent her. It might get him closer to the instigator of Cassandra, the apocalypse.

How can he find out?

How would any spy get information from the enemy.

Stan smiles to himself. With a sense of purpose, the fear releases its hold on him, and his appetite rushes back.

CHAPTER 3
WEDNESDAY

"I'm sorry to have bothered you, Stan." For the third time.

"That's cool." He continues to plug in data fields, instructions to the computer. Numbers and names, letters and symbols stutter up the screen, and are replaced by more.

"I just need to get this report run so I can go through it, fill in my report and, y'know, appease the big-wigs." She laughs a little. It's not nervous as such. Suspicious.

Stan doesn't reply. His eyes hurt but he strains to look at Rachel, keeping his face to the screen. At ease, relaxed.

I've worked out who you are, bitch. "I've set it up to include all computers and telephones."

"That's great! You've not missed anyone out?"

You mean have I excluded myself? "No. Everyone in the company is included in the report."

"Thank you so much Stan. I really am sorry to have bothered you."

"That's cool."

He stands. She doesn't quite block his way. She smiles warmly as he leaves her cubicle. "See you around, Stan!"

He nods. Walks away, a little faster than comfortably, but he hopes she doesn't notice. He's sweating profusely. The sensation of liquid cooling as it rolls down his back and chest. He doesn't want to admit it, but she scares him. Her confidence instills a pervasive doubt in him. His plan will fail. He will be caught. The world will end.

He takes the stairs back down to his floor, like always. Never take lifts. Pragmatism. They can get stuck, they can be turned off, they can break. They're rat-traps for human-sized rats.

He waits out the few hours until he can leave. He doesn't use the computer except to file completed jobs in the appropriate virtual folder on his desktop. He keeps his headphones on, tape playing. No one bothers him.

The office slowly empties. By five o'clock he can feel that there are few people left around him. Picks up bag, turns off monitor.

Through the glass door and on to the marble of the foyer. Rachel. She waits. Lurks in plain sight. He hesitates, turns slightly.

"Stan!" She waves. He pulls his headphones down to rest around his neck.

She must have been waiting for him. The coiling dread awakens again as she walks towards him. Every step a gunshot on the highly polished floor. He winces at each crack.

"I just wanted to thank you so much for your help today." Her smile is disarming. He suppresses the instinct to flinch.

"You're welcome." He leans to pass her. She ignores it. "Good eve –"

"You must let me buy you a drink!"

He stops, shocked. He forces a breath, focuses. No need to panic. This is an opportunity. Something is going his way. He smiles.

Then he feels it. Even separated by tense air, he feels her. Shaking. Adrenaline coursing through her body, causing involuntary shivering. It's not just his opportunity. She is baiting him, trying to draw him to her. Hoping his libido will obscure his reason. Ignorance is a sin.

"A drink. Sure."

"Great! When's good for you? I'm free now…" the invitation hangs there, a verbal bear-trap.

"I can't this week." As an afterthought. "Sorry."

Rachel seems unperturbed. "I have a busy week myself. Going out of town on Friday for a few days. So, how about Monday? Try to kick off the week with a bang?"

"Monday. Sure." He can't bring himself to say it sounds great. A lie too far.

"That's just great. You have a good weekend, Stan." Another of those smiles, disarming and warm. Poisoned honey.

He nods, briefly catches her eyes. They glisten in the clinical light of the foyer. Then he's past her, over the marble and mat and out on to the tarnished concrete. He replaces his headphones. It's drizzling, the tiny drops and spits of rain landing weakly on his face. He pulls up his collar and hunkers down into his coat. He doesn't mind the rain. It drives people indoors. It takes him an hour to reach his flat. He checks over his shoulder at every corner, but does not see Rachel.

Inside, he removes his coat and hangs it up to dry. He turns on the stereo, turns off his Walkman and pauses to let the noise fill the apartment. Changes into dry clothes. Stuffs his shoes with newspaper and puts them in front of his small heater. He fries vegetables, boils rice. While he eats, he plans.

At 7.58pm, he plugs in his television. Before turning it on, he ensures that the curtains are drawn, the door is locked. He turns the light out.

He pushes the button on the front of the black box. The static is audible as it crackles across the glass screen. Waves of color and light shower the room, a confusing jumble of reds, greens and blues. He doesn't need to touch anything else. He only watches one program each week.

Radio static consumes any sound from the television. He has subtitles on. He reads each answer, creates his own question then reads the contestant's response.

"Who was Abraham Lincoln, Alex?"

The credits begin to scroll upwards. He stares at the names and job descriptions floating up the screen. The production company flashes up accompanied by its own fanfare. He leans forward to press the power button. He pauses as an advert brightens the room with blues and yellows. A video rental chain. It is free to join, and there is a local store "near him". He presses the button and the coruscating light is replaced by the shadows and flat, orange glow of streetlights. He unplugs the television. Returns to the armchair. Tomorrow he will pick up some mail and join.

CHAPTER 4
THURSDAY

A city collapsing around him. He stands, unafraid amidst the destruction and cries out against it. His voice is buzzing, the irritating whine of a fly. Darkness swallows the buildings as they fall, until he stands on a small island of asphalt adrift in nothing. He cries out again, raises his empty hands.

Laughter. The screech of machines. The smell of oil.

He is going to die. He cannot see it in the darkness, but he feels it. The means of his death. His buzzing rises in pitch as the deathblow falls.

He is jolted awake by his dream-death. He writes what he can remember on his pad. Slumps back on his pillow. Sleeps again.

Alarm wakes him. He calls work from his house, leaves a message on his boss' voicemail to tell him he is ill. Struggles into his clothes – jeans, t-shirt, sweater and baseball cap (dark blue, with the logo of a baseball team on it) – and heads down the unpainted, warped wooden stairs to the apartment block's hallway.

There are six apartments. Three are unoccupied. One only recently vacated by a black man whose name Stan doesn't know. Stan's mailbox is empty. The black man's is full, the tail-ends of letters jutting from the small slot.

It is still early. Weak dawn light filters through the high, thick panes of glass above the front door. He listens. A faint murmur of traffic. Fragile silence holds the hallway in its thrall. Every sound, every movement Stan makes threatens to pierce the quiet. A nail through ice.

He reaches out with one hand, grasps one of the envelopes. Slowly pulls. It hisses, the echo in the hall transforming the barely audible rasp of papers into deafening susurration. Stan pauses, but all is still. He continues to wiggle envelopes from side to side to ease them out of the over-stuffed box. The first finally comes free. Without looking at it, he pulls on another, the crinkle of the plastic envelope window making him wince.

A small stack of another's mail in hand, Stan retreats up the wooden stairs and back to his apartment. Unlocks the door and slips inside. Twists the various locks behind him and then retrieves a knife from the kitchen. Walks to his armchair and sits. He looks at the top envelope:

```
Tyrell Weyland
Apartment D,
6607 Bay Avenue
13425
```

He dimly recalls that Mr. Weyland was a large black man. No glasses, no hair. Unkempt, with a pervading aura of grease. The perfect choice.

Breakfast. Bread toasted until black. Water. Then he waits. Fires up his computer and connects to the Internet. Before long he is reading memos from the Public Relations departments of the two companies he is watching. Nothing about Cassandra. Nothing that helps him work out who he needs to stop. He does not get frustrated, he is far beyond that. He didn't really expect to find anything. Just killing time.

At 9.38am he turns off the stereo, turns on his Walkman and leaves the apartment again, locking the door behind him. Across the street is a telephone booth. A thick, tatty telephone book is chained to it.

He slides open the dirty glass door and steps inside. The smell of stale urine assaults him. He breathes shallowly, waiting for his nose to grow accustomed to it. Picks up the telephone book. The chain clinks and rattles as he turns over the pages until he reaches **B**. He runs a finger down line after line of small black text until he finds a store in a neighborhood with which he is familiar. He memorizes the street and begins walking.

It is 11.02am when the blue and yellow-framed glass doors slide open and the brief gust of cold, recycled air surrounds him.

Every wall is lined with multi-colored VHS cases, and the store is divided into aisles, each carrying even more. At the top of each bank of shelves is a sign: "Top 10", "Horror", "New Releases", "Comedy". To one side is a blue and yellow counter. A monitor rests on it, a bored looking teenager or university student staring into space as he blows pink bubbles with his gum. His blue and yellow baseball cap is scuffed and sits backwards on his bleached hair. Stan feels uncomfortable looking at it.

Stan removes his headphones and negotiates his way past brightly colored tubs of chocolate and potato chips. The blue floor tiles are cut through with lightning bolts of yellow that hurts his eyes. He fixes his eyes ahead until he reaches the counter. The backwards-cap-kid turns his bleary eyes to almost focus on Stan's face. Stan pulls his own baseball cap a little lower and coughs. Clears his throat.

"Hi. Welcome to Blockbuster Video how can I helpyoutoday?" The kid slurs the words into each other as he pushes them out in one breath. Stan can see the twisted lump of gum coated in saliva as it swills around the employee's mouth while he talks. He squeezes his eyes shut and focuses on his own line.

He smiles to put the employee at ease. Realizes it is effort wasted. The kid is so bored he's barely conscious. Stan wonders if he'd register pain. "I'm working on a paper regarding the depiction of intravenous drugs in modern movies and I was wondering if you could recommend any films that portray this sort of drug abuse?" This is, he reflects, the most he has spoken in perhaps a month. He takes a deep breath to steady himself.

"Uh." Chew, chew. Then, as if Stan has sparked an interest, the kid seems to wake up. His eyes snap in to focus. "Yeah dude. Heard of Pulp Fiction? It's totally rad, and y'know, by the guy who did Reservoir Dogs," Briefly, he sounds human.

Stan stares. Swallows. "Oh, right. That sounds good."

"Awesome dude. I'll totally get it for you right now." He begins to move from behind the counter, then snaps his fingers as if he's just remembered something. "Do you have your membership card?"

"Oh, no. I want to join please."

"Ohhh." The spark fades. "In order for me to process your membership application I'll need two forms of I.D. such as utilities bills or a driver's license." His voice is robotic.

Stan reaches into a pocket, pulls out two utility bills for Tyrell Weyland. The employee – his nametag is bent over at one corner, showing only part of his name *Da* – takes the bills and begins typing on his keyboard. He is slow. Stan takes another deep breath.

One minute and thirty-one seconds later, and *Da* hands him a small blue plastic card. "This is your membership card you will need it to rent videos."

"Sure. Can I get that Pot Fiction now?"

"You mean Pulp Fiction, man. Sure, hang on." He opens the gate in the counter and wanders over to a bank of videos on one wall. His trousers are ripped and baggy. Ridiculous. He returns and hands Stan the video. It is in a blue case with yellow edges. "That'll be two dollars ninety-nine. You pay in advance and have to return it within three days, OK?"

Stan nods and reaches into his pocket. Withdraws a handful of change, sorts it and pays the exact amount. "Thanks."

"Enjoy your movie."

Stan turns to leave. Then, "Oh, dude! If you really wanna some mad drugs skills, hit the movie theater and see

Trainspotting. It's all about heroin and stuff. It's kinda gnarly, but cool." *Da* smiles. His teeth are very white.

"Uh, thanks. Will do." Stan nods and leaves.

* * * *

As he walks home, clutching the blue plastic box to his chest, he keeps his cap pulled low. His eyes scan the sidewalks. Steps over flattened blobs of gum. Avoids the dog-shit while silently wishing death on the scum that let their pets defecate on the street. He is keen to get back to his apartment. He can't help but feel the video case is drawing too much attention. He takes a slightly more direct route home, cutting through areas where he needs to be wary.

As he turns down a street that should skirt a neighborhood he wants to avoid, he sees that a gang of swarthy men fills the street corner. Tattooed skin, black shirts with gold crowns emblazoned on them, low-hanging trousers and pistol grips fill Stan's vision. He turns down the static in his ears to ensure he can hear people around him. He crosses the street immediately, putting distance between himself and this distinct brand of danger.

It is a tragedy that in saving the innocent and deserving, he may also save the rabid dogs that pick on the weak, the parasites that feed on the hard work of people like him. His free hand clenches in to an angry fist. He stuffs it in his jacket pocket. Hides his impotent rage and keeps looking at the street. Hopes that they are too busy to notice him.

"Hey, ven aqui, pendejo!" A shout from the other side of the street. Clearly aimed at him.

Stan's heart begins to pound. He keeps his head down

and keeps walking. The cassette case is growing slick in his hand. He grips it tighter.

Another voice. "Si, ven aqui maricón." Whistling and clucking noises. He tries to see where they are out of the corner of his eye. He sees white and gold sneakers strutting his way. He hunches his shoulders and keeps walking. They're going to stop him, mug him. Maybe stab him. He's going to bleed out on the street and the world is going to die.

A third voice cuts in. "Dejalo en pas, 'mano. He ain't got shit anyway."

Laughter. A bottle shatters a few feet behind him. Stan jumps. Almost drops the case.

The first voice calls out, "Vaya pues, cabron. Run home to mama before I cut your face!"

He does not run, but shuffles, a geriatric sprint, tailed by violent laughter. As soon as he can he turns on to another street. He looks behind him repeatedly as he half-walks, half-runs down it. The video is still clutched in one hand. When he is certain they are not following him, fear is replaced by anger. How dare they? Fucking scum. If he had been ready, if there hadn't been three of them, if... if he wasn't such a coward. He squeezes his eyes shut, but the tears of helplessness and frustration come anyway.

CHAPTER 5
THURSDAY

He has recovered his composure by the time he reaches his apartment block. He opens the heavy front door and pauses. Looks over each shoulder. The street is quiet and he feels safe to go inside. Climbs the stairs to his apartment. Unlocks his door, steps inside and relocks.

He checks his watch. It is 12.05pm. Headphones off. Turns on the radio. Stan leaves the video on his chair and makes himself a sandwich. The bread is a little stale, but still edible. The plastic cheese would survive a nuclear holocaust. He adds some organically grown and carefully sourced tomatoes to his sandwich. They are expensive, but he feels he has deserved it. He cuts the sandwich in half, from one corner to another. The bread sinks slightly beneath his hands. He watches it slowly regain its shape as he carries the small white plate to the chair.

He swaps the plate and video, leaving the former on the chair. He moves to his television and VHS player. He plugs both into the wall sockets and turns the television on. Black and white snow fills the screen. The only sound is calming static from the stereo.

He tugs open the plastic box and withdraws the cassette. The label says "Quentin Tarantino's *Pulp Fiction*". He pushes it into the slot of the VHS player. The machine whirs and ticks. The television screen is black. Small numbers appear in one corner, then a warning in blue and white about illegally showing, copying or distributing the film. Stan retrieves his sandwich from the chair, but sits close to the screen. He does not want to watch the film, doesn't want to follow its plot and characters. He wants to learn from it. He leans forward slightly and presses the ▶▶ button. He fast-forwards through the film.

Minutes pass by and he eats his sandwich while people perform at high speed. He sees a needle and presses ▶. Presses ◀◀ and rewinds a little. Presses ▶. The scene is short, less than two minutes. As the scene changes, he ◀◀ again. Watches blood billowing inside the syringe, then watches the plunger slowly push the mixture of blood and heroin through the skin.

He watches these two minutes seven times before he feels he has learnt all he can from it. He ▶▶ to see if there is more to be seen. There is not. The film's climax is in some sort of roadside diner. As the film fades to black, he presses ■. Rewinds the tape to the beginning, presses ▲ and shuts the cassette back in its box.

He sits. Closes his eyes and tries to envisage the skin of Rachel's arm. It is pale and thin, easily broken by a needle. He chews slowly, ruminating. Before the movie he knew nothing, but his ignorance is merely blunted. There is so much more he needs to know. Perhaps the kid at the video rental store was right and more could be learnt from going to the theater to see a movie that sounds like it has nothing to do with what he needs to know. A movie about trains. He can find no connection, nor can he think of where he could learn more about it, other than to go to a theater and watch it.

Go to a movie theater.

The bread feels like glue, stuck to the roof of his mouth. Somehow it has sucked the moisture from him. He has never been to a theater. Has no idea how to find one or what to do when he is there. He is trapped. The fear of not knowing what to do measured against the fear of facing the unknown. With effort he forces the glutinous ball down.

He'd like time to plan what he will do. He needs to know where he is going, how to get there. He needs to work out the best times to go. But there isn't time to plan.

He brushes the crumbs of his sandwich off the plate and into his small bin. He'll need to empty it soon. A trip that will have to wait. He washes the plate with a half-empty bottle of mineral water that he's left by the sink for this purpose and leaves it to dry.

He wants to change. He shouldn't be seen in the vicinity of the video rental store in the same clothes again. But clothes have always been a problem. He tends to only buy from stores he knows he can trust – hippy clothing, organic fabrics. Subdued colors. The idea of wearing tie-dye makes his skin itch. Not for him. Black, browns and blues. Every day colors, forgettable and indescribable. *He was wearing dark clothing. Blue or black.* Hardly memorable, offering little for anyone to trace. He's not just fighting one corporation. The corporation is part of some secret government program. He is fighting the government. Thousands of men and women sworn to protect and serve the very organization that will destroy them.

He moves to his bed. Underneath are four tray-like boxes. Trousers, shirts and t-shirts, sweaters, underwear and socks. He takes off his sweater, places it on the bed and carefully folds it. Removes another from its tray, this one dark-blue, hand-knitted, and slips it over his head. Soft scratches on his skin as he pulls it down. Places the first sweater into the box and slides it back under the bed.

Stands and picks up his dark blue baseball cap. It is a cheap knock-off he bought from a stall on Canal Street. It is old and frayed along the visor. The band inside is slightly discolored. Time and sweat. He stares at the wavy tidemark. Runs his thumb over it. It is dry, but still he hesitates to put it on. He should get a new one, if he can find someone who sells caps he knows are safe. Until then, he will have to cope. Hiding his face is more important than his discomfort. He unhooks his nondescript dark colored jacket from the hook on the wall and prepares to leave the apartment.

The door's locks slide in to place with a series of reassuringly heavy noises at 1.41pm. The sun is bright, but weak. There is a breeze. It is a typical spring morning. He clutches the blue and yellow box in one hand and walks quickly to the corner of Bay and 324th Street. He pauses. Two yellow taxis pass by. The eyes of the second driver, dirty-looking skin and little hair, flick towards Stan as he drives past.

A chill down his spine. It's possible Rachel informed her

real employers of his absence and the taxi has been doing rounds of the block. He looked foreign, but then didn't most of the taxi drivers he's seen? But no, there is no way they could have found him. He is too careful. His amenities bills do not go to his address but to a Mail Box across town, and he is always careful in his comings and goings. He's still hidden from them. For now.

Nevertheless, he changes direction and takes a more circuitous route back to the video store. This time he sticks to main roads and busy streets. He tells himself it is for anonymity, not out of fear. He is lying. Nevertheless, he will only use these roads. Somehow being surrounded by people makes him feel a little safer. He finds this disturbing.

His route takes him nowhere near the area where he was threatened before. His eyes rove the sidewalk, the asphalt. Try to surreptitiously recognize faces, or imprint features onto his memory. Large nose, a piercing, a mole. It's wishful thinking; the government is hardly going to send a midget with a red Mohican and a face full of metal to follow him. Nevertheless, it gives him something to focus on, to take his mind off recent feelings of impotence.

A car horn sounds and he glances over his shoulder. A yellow taxi. He speeds up a little and ducks under a store awning. Turns. The driver is Asian – Indian or Pakistani – with a large turban. Not the same one as earlier. He continues his walk.

After two hours and eleven minutes he stands in front of the sliding doors to the video store. He can see, through windows streaked with rain and exhaust fumes, that *Da* – is still working inside. Going back in would only draw attention.

Stan loiters. He does not want to go back in. It would be too conspicuous. Then he sees his way out.

To the left of the entrance is a large metal mail flap. Above it, in embossed letters:

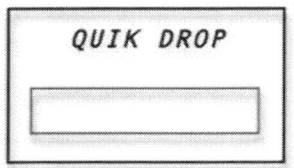

He has already paid his two dollars and ninety-nine cents. The flap must be for people to return videos. It's a liability. Anyone could push anything through. Probably have. He is unwilling to touch the metal with his hands. He pushes the video against the metal slot. Slowly, with the slightest of squeaks, the hinges give and it opens. The video case goes partway through the slot. Stops. The case is wedged between the flap and the metal chute. He wiggles the case, tilts it and angles it so that it tumbles away from him as the flap snaps shut. He quickly pulls his fingers away and steps back.

"Hey man, watch where you're going! Dumbass." The exclamation cuts in over the static of his Walkman.

Stan spins. He has almost collided with a passerby. He mumbles, "Sorry."

The man has already walked away. No one else seems to be paying attention. Stan buries his hands in his jacket pockets, turns up the static and walks down the street looking for another phone box. A block away from the store. He rifles through another tattered phone book for some minutes. Finds a nearby cinema. Starts walking.

There is only one way to reach it. Follow the slow-moving human migration along the main street. Stan moves carefully, avoiding litter on the sidewalk and weaving to avoid brushing against other people. He is acutely aware that he is so much thinner than most of them. Healthier. He does not eat burgers cooked in under a minute. Avoids the dozens of greasy stores claiming to be chicken restaurants, offering patties made from 'mechanically recovered' steroid-injected carcasses. Too many chemicals, too many mind-altering substances could be in them. As well as the fat, bones and brains of animals.

He sways around a woman wearing a poncho as a dress. She is easily three times as wide as him. He is aware that the peculiar stench of her obesity makes his lip curl. He ensures his cap is low over his eyes and keeps walking.

He reaches a T-junction. The building across the street is made of red brick, chrome and neon. Something from the fifties. The names of films are spelled out with red plastic letters on the white board above the entrance: Independence Day, The Frighteners, Trainspotting.

He checks for traffic and crosses the street. The doors are dark wood and large panes of glass, with long brass handles. As he reaches them, a woman pushes open one of the doors and leads a child out by the hand. The child stares at him. Her eyes are wide and dark. She smiles, white teeth and innocence. Stan looks away.

Inside. His shoes make a strange brushing noise on the old, purple carpets. The light is diffuse and unnatural.

He sees no obvious surveillance cameras. He removes his headphones. In front of him is a counter with a high plastic window. Presumably for protection.

He stares at the man behind the window. He is too old to be working in a cinema, selling tickets. Should be in a suit, in a bank. Not in a cheap shirt and bow-tie, not wearing a burgundy vest.

On closer look, the man's glasses are slightly bent. There are stains under his armpits. He has failed to shave properly, and where he has shaved is raw and blotchy. There are numerous pins on his vest. An attempt to look quirky and fun. He looks like a pedophile.

He doesn't speak as Stan approaches him. Just looks expectantly.

"I'd like to see Trainspotting."

"What showing, sir?" The voice is resigned. Waiting to die.

"When is it on?"

The man doesn't need to consult a list or computer, simply looks through Stan as he speaks. "Showings are at 4.45, 7.15 and 9.45."

It is 3.52pm. He will not have long to wait. "Can I see the 4.45 showing?"

"That'll be four dollars and fifty cents."

Stan hands him a ten-dollar bill. The man presses something and a small paper ticket springs up out of the counter. He tears it off and hands it to Stan with his change. Stan stares at it.

"Where do I go?"

The man's smile is wan. "Right up those stairs. You'll find popcorn and soda on the right, and you're in Auditorium Three, which is further along that same side. It won't be open for a while. Enjoy the movie."

Stan refills his head with static. The cinema is reasonably empty. Few people choose to see a film on a Thursday afternoon. His shoes continue to brush across the carpet. He pauses to look at the snack bar. A bored looking college student – short hair, facial piercings, indeterminate gender – leans against a glass counter half-filled with popcorn. Candy and chocolate line the shelves, and two large, glass-fronted fridges house numerous sodas.

There is a warm smell that fills this area. Sweet and comforting. It curls up inside Stan's nostrils. He feels his stomach growl. He stares at the white-yellow popcorn. His mouth feels wetter than it should. He works his jaw to relieve the aching. He recalls the taste from childhood. The texture. Spongy but crisp. The salt and sugar on his tongue. He had only had it once. He can never have it again. Jaw clenched, he turns away.

Beyond the snack bar, the carpeted corridor continues for a short distance. Ends in bathrooms. Two doors are spaced along the right-hand wall, numbered 1 and 3. Number 2 is on the left. There are sofas outside each screen.

He walks to the furthest door on the right and carefully lowers himself onto the sofa. Hands on legs, avoids skin contact with the rough fabric. He perches on the edge and tries to look relaxed. Fails. He dries clammy hands on his jeans.

A couple walks towards him, but turn into Auditorium 1. Three men enter, one after the other. They are not together. All are young.

He stares at the carpet. There is a faded pattern of diamonds. Tiny pieces of popcorn are scattered over dark stains. Memories of human failure. The obligatory grey-black discs of gum.

The dirt, the people, the strange smells of stale popcorn and 'pine fresh' cleaning products swirl around his head. He feels sick. Needs to focus on something else. He counts the tiny popcorn particles. Starts with the crumbs nearest him.

One hundred and eleven before he is distracted. Another cinema employee in a burgundy vest walks up to the closed doors of Auditorium 3 and pushes them open. They do not close, and the employee stands outside. He is young, black. This intimidates Stan. He turns up the volume on his Walkman.

It is 4.39. The black employee is still standing at the door. Stan carefully stands without using his hands. Looks up. The member of staff is speaking to him. Stan removes his headphones.

"Ticket?"

Stan hesitates, nods. He is still clutching the small paper ticket in one hand. He thrusts it towards the burgundy vest. A hand takes it, tears it and then proffers it again. Reluctantly, Stan takes it and stuffs it in a pocket.

"Sit anywhere you like."

"Thanks," his voice cracks slightly. He hurries past and through the open doors, into darkness.

CHAPTER 6
THURSDAY

The darkness is short-lived. The theatre is cavernous and dimly lit. Tiny red lights line the paths between plush seats. To his right, the wall is taken up by a white screen. It is several meters high and perhaps twenty meters wide. The seats are arranged in blocks, those nearest the screen are all on one level, those to his left rise up in tiers.

Above him, the last of the rows of chairs are barely visible in the gloom. Keen to avoid anyone else who might enter, he climbs the stairs. They are low, angled upwards and very long. He cannot find a rhythm. One step up, a step and a shuffle, then another step up.

Music blasts out around him. He jumps. A flickering orange glow throws an immense shadow of himself across the steps. A bizarre fanfare assaults him, reducing static to a quiet buzz. He removes his headphones and quickly ascends to the back row.

The floor at the very back isn't carpeted. There are more

lost and discarded kernels of corn, as well as chocolate and sticky candy. Stan tip-toes to a seat. He chooses one a couple in from the aisle. He is aware what the back row is often used for, and he is sure he can see unpleasant stains further along.

Over the next minute or two, a total of three people enter. Two men and one woman. The men sit together, the woman sits apart from them. Stan watches all three carefully. The woman is slim with curly dark hair. She crams handfuls of popcorn into her mouth and chews noisily. The two men chat and laugh. One has his feet on the back of the chair in front. His shoes are red. Clues to convince Stan of their innocuousness.

The small lights high above him slowly fade to black, and the only light comes from the huge screen. Images of soda bottles and smiling women flash across the screen. Music blares out from speakers around the room. Stan slouches down into his chair, sticks his fingers in his ears.

The advertisement's final scene remains frozen on the screen for some seconds, then fades to black. Stan sits up and takes his fingers out of his ears. There is a mechanical grinding and whirring as the heavy curtains on either side of the screen roll across to cover it momentarily, then roll back. A form is on the screen – black with white writing. It states that Trainspotting has been certified 'R' for Restricted.

This vanishes. Is replaced by thumping drumbeats and to odd-looking men running down a street. A voiceover in a strange accent begins to speak about choice. At least, he thinks it is choice. White subtitles along the bottom of the screen make him think the narrator is not speaking English.

Perhaps he imagined the word choice. No, as the narrator continues to speak about televisions and cars, Stan knows it is in English. But, for some reason, every spoken word is printed on the screen for him. Perhaps this is normal in cinemas, or perhaps he has come to a special showing. Regardless of the reasons, the subtitles allow him to take the headphones from around his neck and put them over his ears. He pulls out the Walkman and turns the volume up to drown out the music and nearly unintelligible dialogue.

It is only two minutes and twenty seconds in to the film when he sees a man with bleached hair tapping the forearm of a woman. She has a belt tied around her upper arm. He is holding a hypodermic needle. There is some talking between the people on the screen, then the bleach-blond man injects her. Stan takes a mental note. He suspects that the belt and tapping are to make the veins more obvious. He continues to watch the film, but avoids reading too much or letting himself focus too clearly on the screen. Just in case.

The comforting white noise accompanies the next twenty-one minutes of the film. Various characters come and go, though the focus is on a young, thin man. He is a heroin addict. Stan waits patiently, hopes for more unintentional guidance.

Twenty-three minutes and thirty-nine seconds in and Stan is suddenly acutely aware of the protagonist kissing a young, attractive woman. In a succession of quick-cut scenes, various couples undress. One woman straddles an unconscious man. A couple embraces on a sofa. Twenty-five minutes and forty-one seconds and the attractive girl is having sex with the thin heroin addict. Her breasts move as she gyrates on him. Stan watches. Fidgets uncomfortably. The act itself looks… sordid. Almost painful. He wonders if he should find it arousing. He doesn't.

He is subjected to two images of male genitalia. He looks away, disturbed and intimidated. The unpleasantnesses are finally concluded two minutes and twenty-nine seconds after he was first made aware of them.

For a moment, thirty-five minutes and twenty-six seconds into the film, Stan sees the bleach-blond man lying on the floor. A syringe is embedded in his forearm, a belt around the higher part.

Eight minutes and twenty-two seconds after this, Stan leads forward. He watches the 'hero' tie a belt around his arm, tighten it and begin tapping the veins of his forearm. A syringe is presented to him. He squeezes it until a tiny bead of fluid is pushed from the needle's tip. A close-up of the arm and its vein. The needle slips under the skin. A small dome of blood forms around the needle, then more seems to gush up the needle and into the syringe. The cloudy mixture is tinged pink. Then he pushes down on the plunger, forcing the concoction into his vein.

Stan wishes he could rewind. Instead he closes his eyes and recalls each stage of the process. Belt, tap, bead, gush, push. He repeats the scene again in his mind.

One hour and twenty-six minutes after it began, and the hero is grinning as he walks towards the camera. He is talking, once again, about televisions and being 'just like you'. Stan smiles. The idiot in the film could not be further from being just like Stan. Stan is in control, he does not give in to ridiculous urges, would not be stupid enough to take drugs or have casual sex. Or sex at all. Too dangerous.

He would not get involved in drug deals, or permit surreal waking dreams to afflict him.

The title of the film appears on the screen in black and white. The narrator – who is also the thin heroin addict (or recovering addict now) is still talking. The film is apparently based on a novel.

The credits roll. Greyscale images of the various actors. The house lights come on again. Stan's eyes ache. He stands, slowly. Avoids his hands touching any surfaces. The other viewers stand and leave. The men talk animatedly. The woman brushes popcorn debris from her short, woolen dress before she descends and walks out.

Stan's legs and back are stiff as he walks back down the awkwardly shaped steps. He turns into the short dark passageway and pushes open one of the doors. It is heavier than he expected. He leans against it with his shoulder to force his way out and into the hall.

One of the two men sits on a sofa near the men's room. The woman has already passed the snack bar. No one seems to pay attention to Stan as he leaves the movie theater. The pathetic man who sold him his ticket has been replaced by a different man, who is busy serving someone.

It is 6.30pm. He does not expect the sun to set for another hour. Plenty of time to get home. He takes a route that takes him through a park, perhaps halfway between the theater and the apartment. The sound of traffic diminishes. The spring evening is chilly. He zips up his jacket and stuffs his hands in his pockets. Feels the small plastic card from the video store. He will need to destroy it at some stage.

The sun is a weak memory of light and warmth by the time Stan turns the final corner and walks to his apartment block. Two cars face each other in the road, the owners shout abuse and blow their horns. Stan doesn't look. Opens the thick front door and slips inside.

CHAPTER 7
FRIDAY

Friday morning. At 8.45am he phones his boss from the payphone. His boss imitates sympathy. He puts the phone down, returns to the apartment and sleeps again to partially repair the damage he inflicts during his week of late nights and early mornings.

11.37am. He's dressed casually and ready to head out. He's got a number of places he needs to visit. No written list. No trail of breadcrumbs.

Careful. He has to be careful. He's laying the groundwork for something big. He cannot get caught. Everything relies on him. He presses play on his Walkman and leaves the apartment.

First stop is a hardware store. Small, independent. Unnoticed. He needs to travel across town. Reluctantly, he takes the subway. Buys a token from the attendant, ensures he doesn't look him in the eye. The peak of his cap keeps his features shadowed. The token is old, worn by hundreds of thousands of hands. The history of it, its promiscuity, makes his fingers ache.

Forty-five minutes later the subway train stops at his stop. He walks up the metal-sheathed steps and into the weak light of early afternoon. The city is grey around him. Buildings, streets, even the people he passes and the light that filters through the clouds seem to have lost their color. But, it is a drabness that has an undercurrent. He can feel it on the back of his neck, almost taste it in the air. The city is waiting. Holding its breath for some act of violence. The electric tension before a boxing match, hidden behind the city's concrete poker face.

The walk from the station to the store does not take long. Once inside, Stan avoids asking for assistance. Unnoticed, unremembered. He browses the aisles, past electrical appliances and gardening tools, ignoring a wall of doorknobs and shelf after shelf of screw and nail.

He finds what he wants and picks up a pack. Unnecessary, as he should need only one. He obfuscates his intentions by picking up a trowel and a pair of gardening gloves.

The attendant is in his late teens. Bored, disinterested. Doesn't even look at Stan as he scans each barcode. Stan pays in cash. Always.

He leaves, stuffing the hardware store's brown paper bag into his backpack. Walks back to the subway, taking a different route.

Metal steps, token, through the barriers and the sliding doors of the subway train. He heads downtown. Twenty-five minutes of noise and rolling and juddering as the old metal trains shudder their way along the decayed arteries of the city.

The sidewalks in this part of the city seethe with life. It heaves and floods around him. He watches feet as they pass by or overtake him. He would hear the dull groan of traffic and the stuttering of feet were it not for the reassuring sound of static in his ears.

The buzz begins to lessen. He reaches into his pocket and pushes the volume up. No change. The batteries are fading, the power and safety they provide is weakening.

For the first time since leaving the subway, he looks up. The drugstore he was looking for is just to his left. The white noise is barely audible, the sounds of the city pressing against his ears.

He runs to the wide glass doors. He is forced to pause as they slide open. He hears the hiss. He looks for the right aisle, but he cannot see a sign. Looks for a shop assistant, rushes towards her.

"Batteries."

"Excuse me, sir?" She is older than a sales assistant should be. Her accent is Mexican.

"I need batteries," he hisses, tries to control his fear. His fists clench and unclench.

Her eyes widen and she steps backwards. "Okay, sir. No problem. What kind of batteries?"

"Batteries! BATTERIES!" He shrieks. The shop immediately stills around him. He can hear the silence. His tape is still playing, but so faintly it is almost drowned out by his breathing. Heavy and panicked.

The Mexican assistant points. He rushes down the aisle. Stops at batteries. Wipes his sweating forehead with the back of his hand. Snatches a four-pack of AA batteries from the racks. Tears the card with hands that shake. Pulls the Walkman out and snaps open the small plastic cover. Turns it over and shakes out the dead batteries before thrusting new ones in. Snaps the cover closed and presses play again. The blast of sound hurts his ears, but he welcomes the momentary pain.

He moves quickly to the counter, waves the torn pack at another assistant and tosses a crumpled note at him. Then he turns and stumbles from the store as quickly as he can.

A security guard moves to intercept him. He sees the boots moving, pausing and stepping aside. The glass doors open and he's back on the street.

He hunkers down into his clothes and walks as quickly as he can to the subway. Buys a token. Takes the first train one stop. Changes to another line. Takes that line three stops. Changes again. Three more stops and he rushes up onto the sidewalk. The city still watches expectantly. He walks, taking side streets and unexpected turns, getting as far away from the drugstore as he can.

Finally he relaxes. He is some miles from where he made the scene. The baseball cap will have hidden him from cameras. Only the shop assistant really saw him. But too many people noticed him, watched his erratic actions. He cannot return there. He needs to find another drugstore.

It is getting dark. He does not have much time left. He checks his watch. Stores will mostly be closed now. He curses quietly. It's too late. His plans will have to wait. Disgusted at his own failure, he turns for home.

He walks for over an hour. It begins to rain, lines of water falling straight down. He feels it soaking through his clothes. Pays it little attention. Rachel has the upper hand.

He will have to wait to see what move she makes. Hope to evade it, or counter it. He cannot make a move yet. He feels the darkness of his dream closing in around him. He wonders if humanity will suffer for his failure.

Something draws his gaze from the water-logged concrete of the sidewalk. A beacon of light. A green cross shining out into the void of the evening. He smiles. Grins.

He checks for cars and crosses the road. The darkness recedes, pushed back by the neon of the twenty-four hour drugstore.

* * * *

The interior is grubby. The linoleum old, cracked. Dirt is wedged in the corners, under the units. He glances at the shelves – plastic bottles, rimed in dust. He does not stop. His destination is the counter. The pharmacist is small, inadequate. Squirms in his own skin.

Stan tries to look calm, natural. Realizes how ludicrous that is. Friday evening, backstreet drugstore. Bad neighborhood. He's too nervous for calm anyway. This place may not sell what he needs.

He reaches the counter. The pharmacist rests one hand on the glass, the other hovers under it. Near a weapon. His eyes are bloodshot.

"Evening, sir." His voice raspy, weak. It suits him. He sounds Jewish.

"Hi." Stan's mouth is dry. He swallows hard. Berates himself for his fear. Pointless worry. "Do you stock insulin needles?"

CHAPTER 8
SATURDAY, SUNDAY

Saturday. He wakes early, jolted in to consciousness by a dream he cannot remember. He scribbles in his pad:

7.17am. Bad dream. No clues.

He lies back. Covers his eyes with one arm. Across the room, on his desk, lie the needles and the cable-ties. He has one more ingredient for his plan to succeed.

He sighs. Today will be difficult. Illegal activities do not sit well with Stan. But, all sorts of things are illegal, not necessarily immoral. What is that saying? Kill one man and you're a murderer. Kill a hundred in a war, a hero.

He showers, dresses. His stomach makes angry, pleading noises. He didn't eat last night. Forces himself to now. Toast, cooked until mostly black. He burns it to remove any possible contaminants. His bin already contains three failed attempts. Drinks water sourced and bottled in Europe.

Never tap.

He turns on his computer. Connects once more to the World Wide Web. They are changing its name, watching in awe as it expands and mutates faster than anyone could have predicted. Already, there are 'online bookshops'. Other industries follow the new trend. Not all are legal. Many 'companies' offer prescription pharmaceuticals, fake visas. A virtualized black market, using the concept of a Global Village to peddle its illegal wares.

He avoids the search engines, works through other channels. He already has an idea of where to look. It isn't hard. Most organizations haven't bought in to the concept of the internet. Only cyber-criminals and cutting-edge gangsters are interested in new communication. Before long, he exhausts his obvious options without success.

Frustrated, he turns to more conventional methods of information gathering. He trawls the search engine results. Finds things under comedy, children and fetish. Nothing matches his needs. Changes tack again. Searches under supplies.

He finds what he's looking for. A quick search provides him a nearby pseudonym that he can use if necessary. The company, like so many others, has not yet stumbled upon the World Wide Web. Stan frowns, checks the address. Walking distance. He scribbles down a telephone number.

He uses the pay-phone across the street. Inserts a coin, dials the number, fingers tapping quickly over the silvery keys, the black paint of the numbers worn away, leaving dull shadows. The phone rings once, twice. A voice, female. He speaks quickly. Her responses are monosyllabic.

"Yes." They have them in stock.

"Yes." He can purchase one today.

"Five." Plenty of time. He puts down the receiver. Looks around. The street is quiet. He crosses back to his apartment building. As he nears the front door, a car glides past behind him, little more than a quiet growl and a sense of movement. He glances over his shoulder. A black sedan.

He freezes. The car is slow as it passes where he stands. Time enough to see him, to mark him. He forces movement, turns to his right, walks away from his apartment and down the street. He takes the first turn into a dead-end alley. He presses against the wall and waits. Nothing. Eventually a blue RV thunders past in the opposite direction.

Stan edges out. The road is empty, the sedan nowhere in sight. He hurries back to his apartment, locks it, slides the bar in to place and ensures the chain is tight. Checks the blinds.

He turns the stereo up, louder than normal. Precaution. He pushes aside a blind a fraction of an inch. No sedan. He is too scared to leave again, to continue with his plans. They are too close, they could learn what he intends. He cannot allow that.

He spends the rest of the day and the night at the window, interrupting his vigil only to eat and urinate. He does not even attempt sleep.

* * * *

Sunday. He leaves the house early. 7.54am. Dressed casually, baseball cap low over his eyes. It is a grey day, without heat, but not cold. No subway this time. Instead he walks in the opposite direction to the center of the city. As soon as possible he turns off the main road and begins picking his way through narrow streets and detritus-strewn alleyways.

The city is piled on top of itself. A child clutching at its own body, scared to stretch or fill space. It is a short walk from quiet, residential streets to one of the various industrial areas. The tall houses, set back from the sidewalk, their doors raised up by steps, end abruptly. He crosses tarmac, and on to cracked concrete, hemmed by chain fences, crumbling husks of buildings. Echoes.

The factories, old, broken and shabby, are indelible pockmarks on the city's face. He moves between them along cracked roads, the yellow lines worn away to pale pastels. Most are abandoned, but some struggle on despite infirmity. The sounds of old machines, the predecessors of the apocalypse, reach his ears. He turns up the volume on his Walkman.

Three small black metal bollards mark the border between industrial and inhabited. The concrete and brick wrecks are replaced by renovations, by wrecks that have been rebuilt. Workhouses repackaged as luxury. Instead of broken concrete, trendy nightclubs and bijou restaurants line cobbled pedestrian paths.

Face down, he continues. It is 9.28am when he reaches the store. It is between a stationery store and a mini-mart. Its front is white and blue.

Inside smells clean, crisp. The air conditioning unit whirrs contentedly above him. The racks of medical supplies divide the room into several aisles, all leading inexorably to a cheerful oriental girl at the counter.

"*Good* morning!" She sounds rich. Med student. "How

can we help you today?"

"I – " he swallows. "I'm looking for some scrubs."

"O*kay*, that's no problem at all, sir. Do you know what size you are?"

He had not thought of this. He does not know his size. He wants to take off his cap and jacket. It is suddenly hot.

The oriental girl – her nametag says Kathy – continues, seemingly unaware of his pause. "You look like a medium to me. Here, let's see."

She leans under the counter. Straightens and places two cellophane-wrapped, folded blue bundles in front of him.

"These should be your size."

Stan nods his agreement. His smile is mostly genuine, though driven by relief. "Perfect. Thanks."

"Hey, no problem, sir. That'll be ten dollars and ninety-nine cents."

Stan reaches into his pocket, hands her a crumpled ten-dollar bill, and counts out the exact change.

"So, you must work over at Saint Vince's, huh?"

Stan nods absent-mindedly.

"Yeah, I'm hoping to do my residency there."

Stan hands her ninety-nine cents in change, forces a less convincing smile. "Good luck. It's a great place."

She smiles widely, opens the till and drops coins into various compartments. Puts the scrubs into a paper bag. "Have a great day, sir."

"Thanks." He takes the paper bag. An afterthought, "You too."

CHAPTER 9
SUNDAY

10.09am. Stan watches people enter and leave through the over-sized sliding doors of St. Vincent's hospital. Their faces are blank, uniform. He couldn't pick any one of them out of a line-up. They might as well be ants. His eyes pass over them as they march.

He got changed in a nearby alley. His clothes are stored in a dumpster. He waits, drinks bottled water from Europe. He leans against a rough brick wall, tries to remain inconspicuous. It isn't that hard, especially here. People pay no attention to those around them. They are fixated with themselves. And scared to look around, afraid of what they might see. So, he loiters, dressed in his blue hospital outfit. Studiously ignored.

He does not have to wait long. At 10.51am he hears a siren, a quiet, background wail. In moments, it is a piercing whine as the ambulance skids to a halt. Even as it turns off the siren, another ambulance shrieks into the area in front of the hospital. Doctors and nurses in blues, whites and greens rush out. Soldier ants swarming out to defend the hive from threat, crawling all over the paramedics and the broken, bloodied things they pull from their vans.

Stan moves his headphones to around his neck. He can still just barely hear the white noise. A necessary risk. He keeps his cap on. He has seen various medical staff come and go with hats on. He jogs over, grabs one of the gurneys and helps push it through the sliding doors. The air conditioning's synthetic breeze slips over him.

The man on the trolley does not move. His eyes are barely open, his mouth forced into slack-jawed gaping by the breathing tube. Someone's hand squeezes the bag, sending air into the man's lungs. His face is bloodied, his bare torso scraped and red. A glance lower reveals a bloody ruin where hips and legs should be.

Stan remains quiet as a balding paramedic reels off statistics to a young doctor as she directs the gurney through another set of double doors and towards an operating theatre.

"RTA. Biker scissored by a beemer and a civic. Vitals are shit, BP dropping fast…"

The young doctor cuts him off, "Get me four units of O Neg, and clear Trauma Room Three. Now!"

Stan lets go of the gurney, but keeps pace until it is pushed through the double doors of trauma room three. They swing back towards him, and he veers away along a corridor. Various medical staff rush around him. He keeps his eyes down as he slowly walks past discarded beds and wheelchairs, the unpleasantly sterile smell of the hospital heightening his sense of unease. He hopes his discomfort is not as apparent as he feels it must be.

His shoes quietly squeak on the dark blue floor. A nurse runs past him, keys jangling. She stops at a door marked 'Staff Only'. Shuffles through her keys. Stan slows his pace, walks behind her as she finds the right key and unlocks the door. As she walks in, it slowly closes behind her. Stan stops, crouches by the wall. Fumbles with his shoelace. Seconds pass and the door opens again. The nurse emerges, clutching two glass vials and some gauze bandages. He tenses. She looks the other way, hurries down the corridor. In two quick steps Stan is inside the room.

It is dark inside, rapidly becoming black as the light of the corridor is obscured by the door. His hand scans the wall before his fingers find the switch. He flicks on the light. Rows of bandages and plastic bags lie dormant on shelves. Glass cabinets are stocked with tubes and bottles.

He does not waste time. He will have precious little of it before discovery. He opens cabinets and wall units, searches for some sort of order. He twists various bottles to reveal complicated names he does not understand. His search becomes increasingly frantic. The first cabinet is useless.

The second, however, contains morphine, Vicodin and Percocet variants. He moves aside some of the newer medicines, trendy narcotics. Picks up the vial he is looking for and tucks it into his pocket.

Turning the lock, Stan opens the door. Flicks off the light and steps into the corridor. Staff strut past him, patients drift along the blue hallway. He feels his face twisting. He is surrounded by the weakness of humanity, resignation. A forced defiance against death fails to hide it. He swallows scorn. Fidgets with his cap, pulls it lower. Wipes the sweat from his forehead. Walks.

Along the corridor. He looks into Trauma Room Three. The biker is all but naked. A small woman holds defibrillators up at her shoulder height. He hears her faintly through the doors. "Clear!" She presses the metal pads to his chest, pushes. The body jerks once, lies still again. Blood, dark and viscous, drips lazily to the tiles. Nurses try to stem its exodus for a few seconds, before stepping away as the doctor raises her pads menacingly.

Stan turns away, setting his headphones over his ears once again, surrounding himself with the safety of static. The sliding doors are in constant motion. Each attempt to close foiled by the flow of the sick and the lame. Stan walks quickly, with purpose. He belongs. Ignore him. He is busy.

Neither staff nor patients spare him even a glance. He walks across the waiting area, past the reception. He feels the push of cold air on his neck. The doors are open. He mentally counts down the steps until he is outside.

Into daylight. He smiles to himself, turns to face the alleyway. It shouldn't be this easy.

A hand on his shoulder. "Excuse me, sir."

The hand is too heavy. Stan feels its weight fixing him in place. He struggles to stay upright. Fear steals his strength.

"Sir?"

Stan fights against the gentle tugging. Realizes that he cannot shrug the hand away. Must not. His hopes of going unnoticed have withered. He prays to a god he knows does not exist that he will somehow escape.

Stan lets himself be turned as he removes his headphones again. Faces the security guard. He is shorter than Stan expected. Without a uniform. He looks concerned. Nervous. His red tie has an old stain ground in to it.

"Sir, I'm looking for my son. Could you help me please?" The man's eyes are laced by tiny veins, the lids red and raw-looking. He has a day's growth of white stubble.

Not a guard, then. Someone lost. Stan's held breath tumbles from him. Ragged and relieved. Uncertainty follows. Refusal might result in hurled abuse, attention-drawing shouts. But, agreeing to help, only to demonstrate ignorance of the hospital's geography, could likewise be catastrophic. He can't run. Fine then, a bluff. He can pretend to be someone else. He can act the part. He nods.

"Thank you, thank you, doctor."

"Nurse."

"Oh, sorry, uh, nurse."

Stan pulls his mouth into a smile. "What did you say your son's name was?"

"Jacob. Jacob Warchowski."

"And, do you know why he's here?"

"He was," the man pauses, swallows. "He was brought in in an ambulance. The hospital called, but it's so busy in there, I can't find anyone to help. I saw you leaving and thought..."

Stan nods again, refuses to let his cheeks relax. "OK, mister Warchowski, follow me."

Swish of the oversized doors, ineffectual push of the air conditioning. He walks across the laminated flooring he'd hoped to never see again. He can hear the lost Warchowski scampering behind him. The smell of the man's fear overpowers the hospital's sterility.

The nurse at the reception desk is tired. Her face sagging,

unable to combat gravity and the misery of being surrounded by the sick and dying. Her rheumy eyes peer at Stan over her half-moon glasses.

"Yes?"

"This gentleman is looking for his son. Warchowski. EMT brought him in – " he glances at the father. "When did you get the call, sir?"

"Only ten minutes ago. I work just down the street. In a" – his voices dwindles – "dry-cleaners." He hangs his head. Knows that now, especially now, his job is an irrelevance.

The nurse scans a chart. "Warchowski. Warchowski. Ah yes, RTA. Trauma Room Three. I would suggest that Mister Warchowski Senior waits in the waiting room. A doctor will be along as soon as possible."

"Why? What's happened? Is he all right?" The man's eyes are obscenely wide. His terror is an unpleasant stain in the air.

Stan steps between the counter and the lost soul. "Come with me, sir. Your son is going to be fine."

"No! Tell me, please! What's going on?"

"I'll tell you what I know, but you need to sit down. Creating a scene will have you thrown out." The vial is an ever-present barb in his pocket.

The lost soul withers, walks to a plastic bucket-seat and slumps in it.

Stan sits next to him. Perches on the edge of the seat. Doesn't want to catch anything. "Your son was involved in a road-traffic accident. He was brought in here with quite serious injuries."

Those obscene eyes again. "Will he be ok?"

"I'm sure he will. The doctors were working hard to help

him as I left. Now, you are going to have to wait here until someone comes to talk to you. It won't be long."

Sniff. "Thank you. I will."

Stan nods. Swallows the words he's longing to voice. The man's life is irrelevant. This building is irrelevant. It is rubble. They are smears of blood and bile. Unless Project Cassandra can be stopped. Unless Stan can stop it.

Instead, he says, "I'm going to go now." He stands and walks away. He does not look back. One ant, hundreds of ants. Who's counting?

He has billions to save. Billions of ungrateful ignorants. The martyr's curse.

The squeak of plastic-coated flooring, the breath of cold air, the swish of doors and he's back in the comfort of the streets and, as he replaces his headphones, static.

Head down, he walks away from the hospital, to the alley and his clothes. Hiding behind it, he changes quickly. Removes the vial, slips it into his jeans. Places the scrubs in the bag. Leaves the alley. Heads for home. After forty-two minutes, he changes his mind. He has one more task.

He takes the subway West as far as it goes. Leaves the station. A short walk and he is surrounded by dirty scrubland. Pale grass and dust. Abandoned construction sites and forgotten factories. Large drums, cardboard homes, the smell of stale alcohol and piss.

Bodies are heaped around him. A living holocaust exhibit. A mass grave for those dead who haven't yet realized their fate. Occasionally, one of the corpses moves. Rolls, tugs sodden cardboard over its unkempt head.

He turns off his Walkman, removes the headphones. Comforting white noise replaced by the sounds of lethargy.

Shuffling, coughing, the faint crackle of fire. Seagulls. And, distantly, traffic. Life continuing, obstinate in its ignorance.

Most of the metal drums are cold, whatever fuel used up. He ignores these. One still burns, tended by an ancient woman in three coats and a headscarf. Her smell is overpowering. Alcohol, an alcoholic's incontinence, decades of filth. Stan covers his mouth. An unconscious act. A weakness.

The ground around the drum is a carpet of near-humanity, dead rats and accumulated refuse. He steps carefully over those who sleep huddled around the fire. They are filled with a chill only booze can melt, but the fire dulls it. He feels only scorn. He wonders again why he bothers.

The crone's eyes are dull. She looks at him, sees his bag. Taking his hand from his face, he pulls out the scrubs and her gaze leaves him, looks through him. He has not brought her anything of interest.

He dumps the scrubs into the fire. Remembers the video store card in his pocket. Pulls it out and reads it again. Tyrell Weyland's name is printed in black ink on the blue plastic. He tosses it into the flames. Watches as it and the scrubs are consumed. Blue wavering, melting and glowing before blackening. Crumbling in on itself. Like a building. A body. He cannot help but see the cycles, the constant mimicry. Death imitating life imitating death.

He watches the flames. He is uncertain for how long, but it is 12.06pm when he turns away. The crone looks at him again. As he walks back to the subway, he wonders if she is begging him to kill her.

CHAPTER 10
MONDAY

He's at a house party. The house is a wooden building on the beach. It has too many stairs and hallways, and no rooms. Or, if there are rooms, he cannot find them. He is dressed as a knight. No one else is wearing a costume. His embarrassment is a burning sensation all over his body. All around him are people. They are young, intertwined, dancing to music he cannot hear. They are faceless.

Then he sees her, disappearing through the tangled throng of people. He calls out to her, but he has no voice. He struggles through the web of people, pushing past dancers and drinkers and lovers. He silently shouts again. See her disappearing downstairs. He follows, shouldering the anonymous partygoers aside until, for a reason he cannot understand, he walks slowly down a wooden staircase. To the basement door.

He opens the door and steps out on to the beach. It is night, the moon is heavy and low above him. He walks around the house, searching for her. Sand sprays as he walks, silvery bow waves around his feet. Dunes rise on his left, multi-colored flashes through the windows of the house on his right.

He is facing the door. Looks up and sees her. She is looking down at him through a window. Monochrome in the moonlight.

He waves at her. She waves back. He sees her smile. He is happy.

Then, without warning, without reason, the ground trembles beneath him. He feels the sounds of machines in the earth beneath him. The shrieking. Flames are pushing up through the sand, clawing up the dried wood of the house. The dancing becomes jerking, spasmodic. A Wicker Man in offering to the weapons of the apocalypse.

The house is ablaze. Silent screams assail his ears. He looks at the window. She is standing there, serenely. She is waving. The flames climb to the window. The house is collapsing, the fire consuming wood and flesh.

The fires reach her. The world is orange and yellow, heat and smoke. She is vanishing behind flames and crumbling wood. Still she is waving to him. She is smiling. She is smiling.

Stan lurches awake. He is dimly aware that he is shouting. His throat is raw. Sweat coats his body like a second skin. He reaches for the bottle of water by the bed. His hands are numb and the bottle falls to the floor.

"Shit," his voice sounds alien to him. He picks up the bottle and drinks. Gulps down the cool liquid. It hurts to swallow, but he continues, quenching the burning panic in his gut. He takes up his pencil and pad and tries to make notes about the dream. Finds the images disturbing and writes only in the vaguest terms.

It is 4.18am. He turns his pillow over and lies his head on the cool fabric. He closes his eyes. The darkness behind his lids is peaceful. He begins to fall back to sleep.

She is smiling.

The image flashes before him. He winces and opens his eyes. He does not know what the dream means. This was no epiphany. Most concerning is that he dreams of Rachel at all. Why does he chase her? Why should he care about finding her? She is a threat. Subtle and insidious. Another obstacle placed in his way. Nothing more.

He closes his eyes again and drifts to sleep.

She is smiling.

CHAPTER 11
MONDAY

Monday morning. Stan wakes, dresses. He makes his lunch, before preparing his breakfast of toast, cooked until all impurities have been burnt away. The smell of its burning reminds him of his dream. He throws it away. He removes the garbage bag and ties it closed.

Turns off his stereo, turns on his Walkman. Leaves the apartment. He walks two blocks North and drops the bag in a dumpster in an alley behind two restaurants. From there he walks to the office. His walk is shorter than usual. He is distracted by his dreams. Disquieted.

Concrete, mat, marble. In to his office. He turns on his computer, stares at the requests for help from without reading them. They are irrelevancies. His mind is filled with, overwhelmed by, the problem of Rachel. The problem of dealing with the problem.

He stares through his computer screen for the first thirty-six minutes of his day. People walk past and around his desk. None greet him.

At 9.37am, his eyes snap back into focus. He is uncertain what he was thinking about. This worries him. He cannot afford these lapses. He removes his headphones. He is surprised no one has admonished him for wearing them. Perhaps, ironically, he is beneath their notice.

He has received an email from Rachel. He clicks his mouse twice and opens it. It asks how his weekend was and what time does he finish work.

He remembers now. He agreed to a drink. He has not brought the things he requires. He cannot do what he needs to tonight. His head is in his hands. He breathes deeply. Fights the urge to scream and ineffectually pound the desk. He's fucked. He has to go for drinks with an attractive woman. A woman who wants him dead. He has to chat and charm her and, over the course of the evening, somehow convince her she would want to meet him again.

He has never had drinks with a woman. He's never had drinks.

Replies to her email. His weekend was ok, thanks. He finishes at five. Where would she like to go for a drink? Clicks send.

He finds a document accidentally saved in the temporary folder for some moron on the third floor. Replaces the toner cartridge on the first. Returns to his desk. There is another email from Rachel in his inbox. It was sent to him at 10.13am.

```
Re: Weekend.
Five's great for me. I'll meet you in the foyer.
I've heard Safari across the road is good. Or, we
can try that bar on 3rd. D'Amico's?
```

R x

He does not reply immediately. He works until 12pm exactly. He does not eat lunch in the office. He leaves and walks across the street to Safari.

The exterior is black glass and white framing. The inside is fake zebra-skin seats, black tables and African ornaments. The lighting is weak, dim. Lighting to hide by. As he removes his headphones, the sounds of conversation mingle with odd tribal beats.

The striped bar itself runs the length of the back wall. There is no clear path to it so Stan is forced to walk between tables. Few are occupied, and those that are, by men and women in business attire.

He threads his way to the bar. The bartender is polishing the black counter with a damp rag. He is thin, clean-shaven. His white shirt is crisp. Stan cannot see his eyes in the half-light. This makes him nervous.

"Do you have mineral water?" Stan stands near, but not touching the bar. The rag is grey. It leaves a trail of tiny smears in its wake.

"Yeah. Still an carbonated." His accent has a foreign lilt. He does not look up as he speaks. The rag continues to sweep wetly across the slick black surface.

"What kind is it?"

"Still. Or carbonated." The droplets slowly dry, leaving small dirty stains.

"I mean, what brand is it? What's the name on the bottle?"

The rag pauses. Small eyes peer at Stan from under dark brows. "What?"

"Um, what brands of bottled water do you sell?"

The bartender leaves the rag and walks to the far end of the bar. Squats down. Stands and walks back.

"Pinnacle. It's called Pinnacle. Still or carbonated. White or green glass. Any other questions, or you gonna buy a drink?"

Pinnacle. A famous, established American brand. A brand he knows cannot be trusted.

"Thanks." He walks away, weaves between tables and chairs and heads for the door. He slides his headphones over his ears, blocking out any abuse the bartender might send his way.

Back on the street. He walks towards 3rd Avenue. Three blocks. He stops outside an old-fashioned building. Red, white and green awnings above sturdily built wooden tables and chairs. The door squeaks quietly.

The large windows at the front illuminate the inside. More tables and chairs on wooden floors. He removes his headphones. Sinatra replaces static. An Italian flag hangs proudly but limply above the bar on one side of the room. The bartender is leaning against the bar, looking bored. Striped shirt, open too far, and a gold medallion. His eyes are puffy, and fix Stan with a look that is neither wary nor welcoming. His hair is slicked back. A fat Italian Elvis impersonator.

"Wad can I git ya, spoyt?"

"What bottled waters do you sell?"

"Bahdled wuhduh?"

"Yes."

He turns and pulls a thick, green glass bottle from a shelf. "San Nicolo. Soysd and bahdled in Idahly."

"Italy?" Safe. Perfect. "Thank you." He tries not to sound too relieved.

"Yuh wuhn id?"

Stan shakes his head. "I'll be back later."

"OK bud."

On to the streets. White noise for the three blocks. He stops at an ATM machine. Uses the card registered to an address he's never visited. Withdraws twenty dollars. This should be enough for a quick drink with a spy. He goes into a nearby local store, exchanges the twenty for two ten-dollar notes. Walks half a block. Exchanges the two ten dollar bills for a used twenty in a hardware store. Back to work. Concrete, mat, marble.

At his desk, he removes his cheese sandwich from its small plastic bag, turns off his headphones and checks his email. His stomach clenches until he sees nothing from Rachel.

He washes down his sandwich with some French water, goes to the bathroom. Into a cubicle. Lifts the seat, fingers hidden behind paper. Urinates. Flushes and washes hands. Back to his desk.

It's 1.03pm. He has less than four hours to prepare himself for his meeting with Rachel. It is not a date. It can't be a date. He is not sure he'd be able to go on a date, even if he wanted to. And he does not want to, not with her. Not with a spy.

He is kept busy for most of the afternoon by a server problem. Important men and women come to him to moan and pester. Executives, directors, vice-presidents. People whose jobs will not exist soon, fretting about work that will be nothing but ashes and memory.

He considers ignoring them, but he needs the money. It pays for his internet access, his apartment and his food. So, he bears the assault on his ears, the near-hysteria that uncertainty evinces. It takes two hours and twenty-four minutes to resolve the problem. Nothing has been lost; it was all stored safely. No one thanks him.

He has numerous jobs outstanding. He doesn't even look at them. He spends ninety minutes running over conversation topics and compliments. "You look nice." "How about this weather?" "How is work going?" He sounds ludicrous, even to himself. Might as well ask "What about that Unabomber?" He whispers and discards subject after subject, loathes every fawning platitude.

At 4.57pm Stan returns to the bathroom. Urinates purely out of nervousness. Washes his hands and looks in the mirror. His eyes look fear-filled. He runs his hands through his hair. Tries to smooth it down. Fails. Sniffs under his arm. Acceptable.

On the other side of the open-plan office, Rachel is standing by his desk. Her coat is folded over one arm, and she is looking around the office. Looking for him. He stops, watches for a moment. Is she checking his computer? There's nothing on it that could interest her, but seeing her looking would confirm his suspicions. She is still standing placidly at his desk thirty seconds later. He is shaking slightly as he walks over.

"Hey!" She smiles warmly.

"Hi."

"Are you ready?"

"Yes. Uh. Let me get my bag."

"Sure thing. Did you decide where you wanna go?"

Stan nods. This is already a nightmare. "D'Amico's?" It turns in to a question. Almost pleading. Pathetic.

"Great! I've heard good things."

He ensures that his computer is off and gathers his bag and jacket. They leave together, and he is aware that eyes follow them. Co-workers watching him leave with a woman. More likely, watching Rachel leaving with a man they've not noticed before. His shoulders rise as he hunkers down and speeds up, keen to escape notice. Stan tries to focus on what Rachel is saying, tries to listen over the sound of blood rushing through his head.

"…and so I couldn't believe when I saw the amount of calls to numbers that weren't business-related. It's been pretty slack, you know? So I've put in my recommendations to Bob – you know Bob? Bob Travers, up on the third – and hopefully he'll send out a note to everyone to watch their phone use."

"Mm." He doesn't know what to say. He has no fucking clue who Bob is. He's never used the work phone to make a personal call. He doesn't have anyone to call anyway. He could call his mother, but he doesn't know her number.

Rachel's still talking.

"I told her she should just go for it, you know? I mean, what's the worst that could happen? It's hardly going to be the end of the world if he says no is it? What do you think, Stan?"

Shit. "Yeah." They've travelled less than a block. He is missing the comforting sound of white noise. He has not travelled outside without it for a very long time. He has to interrupt her.

"—knew you'd agree. You're like me, you tell it how it –"

"Rachel?"

"Yeah?" She glances at him, still smiling.

"I forgot something. I need to go and grab it."

"Oh, OK." The smile falters. Something inside him twinges.

"I'll meet you there. I won't be long." He walks back. Quickly crosses the street and then turns to look. She has continued walking. He withdraws his headphones from his bag and puts them on. Presses play. Breathes deeply as the familiar noise floods his ears. Safe. It allows him to think, to focus.

He has taken too many risks already. He needs to be careful or they will find him. Rachel may have already told them to watch the two places. He hopes that D'Amico's is busy. It's public at least, so he should be safe. He needs to ensure that next time, when he's prepared to do what needs to be done, it's on ground he knows. Somewhere he can hide from them if they're watching.

For now, no choice. Drink water, avoid food and be charming. Just another test he must pass. For humanity's sake.

He waits behind a Ford Pick-Up for a minute or two. Crosses the street again and walks to D'Amico's. At the door he removes his headphones, turns off the Walkman and hurries inside.

It is busier than at lunch. The tables at the front of the bar are occupied by business people in sharp suits. The further in he goes, and suits give way to shabbier clothes. Probably students. In a far corner, a few tanned men, dressed like the bartender in shirts that are too open, are gathered. They are playing cards and muttering to one another.

Stan notices one man, sitting near the door. Alone, reading a newspaper. Occasionally writing. Is he writing notes? Stan freezes, panicking. He is certain that the man – plain-looking, middle-aged, eyes hidden behind glasses – is watching him. A glance towards Stan, then back to the paper. Panic. What does he know? What does Stan do?

The man chews on one end of a pen before pulling it from his mouth and scribbling something down on the paper. Pen back to mouth. To paper. Stan watches for a few more seconds. The man's gaze never leaves the paper. Pen to paper. Then, casually, paper on to table. The crossword is completed.

It could be that he has made notes in the boxes of the crossword, but it is unlikely. He can see that each box is filled by a letter, and there are not enough boxes for anything useful to be written there. His shoulders un-hunch, slightly. He scans the room for Rachel.

She is sat at a table halfway along the wall opposite the bar. Her chair faces the bar, his will face her. His back will not be to the street, thankfully.

She sees him and smiles. He pulls the corners of his mouth towards his eyes and walks to the table.

"Get what you needed?"

"Yes, thanks." A pause. What to say next? "Would you like a drink?"

"I'll have a gee'n'tee. I could do with one."

"Okay. I'll be right back."

In four short steps he is at the bar. The same Vegas-years Italian bartender. If he recognizes Stan, he doesn't show it. Suspicious ignorance.

"Wad'll id be spoyt?" His eyes are flat. He has no recollection of Stan. Good.

"A bottle of San Nicolo still water and a tee'n'gee."

The bartender huffs air out of his nose like a bull. "You mean gin an tonic?"

Gin and tonic. Of course. Stan nods. "And a bottle of San Nicolo. Still."

"Comin'rideup."

Stan almost rests one arm on the bar in an attempt to look relaxed. Look like he belongs. He feels ridiculous. The bar looks unclean and sticky. He cannot quite lean on it. Cannot allow his clothes to touch the filth staining the wood.

The bartender places a green bottle in front of Stan on the bar, followed by a glass with several blocks of frost-furred ice. Then a narrow, straight glass filled with ice and the colorless alcohol. Already the cubes are slick and smooth looking, so unlike his.

"Nine-fifty."

Stan fishes in his pocket. He had thought that a twenty would have paid for the evening. Had not anticipated the cost of drinking water downtown, had not anticipated being forced to pay so much because he wanted to drink in a bar. He hands over the note, waits for the change. The bartender hands him a mix of notes and coins and turns away. Stan stashes the money in his pocket and wipes his hands on his trousers. He will get rid of it as soon as possible.

He reaches out his hands towards the glasses. Stops. He has no idea how he is going to carry everything. How do other people manage it? He wraps his thumbs around the bottle, draws the two glasses close to it with his fingers. He presses them together and lifts, but the glasses and bottle slip against each other. He rearranges, thumbs and forefingers around the bottle, his hands around each glass. A gentle clink as he lifts. A tight smile of victory.

Slowly, he turns and makes his way back to the table. His eyes are fixed on the liquid as it sloshes while he walks. The ice cubes continue to chime quietly, bubbles trickling up their sides.

He bends and places the glasses and bottle on the table. The ridges of the bottle scrape against the scars of the wood. For some reason, the noise sets his teeth on edge.

"Thanks, Stan! You ok?"

He realizes he is grimacing. Nods. "Fine, hope I got your drink right."

Rachel makes a noise. A squeal mixed with a hiccup. "Oh you're so funny! As if you'd get that wrong." She squeaks again.

"Heh. Yeah. Right."

Someone behind him laughs. Stan starts. Looks over his shoulder. Are they laughing at him? Do they know something? He feels exposed. The butt of jokes he cannot hear. A feeling nauseating in its familiarity. Men as boys, boys as rats.

Whimper concealed by the croak of wood-against-wood. Chair pulled back. He slumps into it. His back is damp.

"I know how you feel. Been a long week."

Jesus. He'd almost forgotten she was here. Straightens in the chair. Runs a hand down his face. Reaches for the bottle of water. Ignores the glass. Drinking from a glass is dangerous. Germs, contamination. Infections, physical and mental.

Twists the cap off and raises the bottle.

"Cheers!" Rachel lifts her glass towards him.

"Uh. Cheers."

Clink.

He drinks deeply from the bottle. Places it back on the table. Breathes.

She is smiling at him. Her eyes are sparkling. Mocking?

"So…" she pauses. Expectant.

This is it. He feels his legs shaking. Nerves. Not because of who she is, what she represents. No. For some reason, some unfathomable reason, he wants to impress her.

"So…" he replies. "You were saying?" He means droning. Incessantly and pointlessly.

"Oh, nothing important. How was your day?"

"Uh. Fine, I guess."

"Don't you get frustrated with all these people who just can't work a computer? I mean, how hard is it to plug in a mouse?"

Stan almost narrows his eyes. Suspicious. "What do you mean?"

Her smile is unwavering. "You know, all these guys in the office, so smart and fulla themselves, but they can't even turn on a monitor. They're like, 'duh, the TV is black. How do I make it work?'" She laughs. Squeaky. Somehow, endearing.

He scowls. Forces a cough he hopes sounds like laughter. "Morons," he says. Idiots and fuckwits. Not just people at work.

"I *know*, right?" She squeaks some more. "Oh, Stan. You're so funny!"

He has no response. No idea why she says that. He drinks water in lieu of witty retort.

Sudden light and noise from the bar. Television. Rachel gestures to the screen with her head. "You a devils fan?"

Stan glances over his shoulder. His hand stays on the bottle, thumb over the lip so she cannot slip anything in to it. Ice Hockey.

"Gotta love them Devils," she says. He thinks she is being sarcastic, but isn't sure. He looks back at her. Smiles weakly.

"You'da thought after last season they'd be kickin' butt."

"Yeah."

"So, not a big sports fan, huh?" She leans forward. "So, what *do* you like, Stan?"

"Uh, Jeopardy?"

She lifts one eyebrow.

His face is burning. "The show where the answers are questions."

She grins. "Oh, I know it." She sings the timer tune. *"Dum dum dum dum, dum dum dum dum. Dum dum dum dum,"* her finger points up for the high note, *"dum dumdumdumdum."* She laughs.

He is horrified. She is singing in a bar. People are looking. He can feel the weight of strangers' regard. Stifling him. He is dimly aware that he is tugging his shirt away from his throat.

"What?" She is still laughing. A studied act in carelessness. Infuriating. Engrossing.

"Nothing. Just not used to – to singing in public. That's all."

"Oh, well, get used to it. Next week I'm taking you to

Karaoke!"

Silence. His brain is screaming in panic. He chokes on air.

"Relax! I was joking. Sheesh, Stan, you need to lighten up!"

Somehow, she constantly has him reeling. He needs to assert control. Learn about her. This has to go well if he is going to see her again. If he is going to find the opportunity to do what must be done. He thinks back to the two films he has watched. Both were for a different sort of education, but perhaps he can dredge up something else. The hitman and the gangster's wife, on a date. Milkshakes. Dancing.

"Foot rubs."

"What was that?" She looks blankly at him.

"Uh, I said, know any jokes?"

"Hmm, not any good ones. What's green and stands in the corner?"

Stan shakes his head.

"A naughty frog."

Silence. She looks at him, grinning. Waiting.

"Geddit?"

He barks out a laugh. It sounds painfully fake in his ears. "A naughty frog. *Ha!*"

She laughs again. "I can't believe you found that funny! Your turn now."

"I don't know any jokes."

"Of course you do! Everyone knows a joke!"

He shakes his head. "The only joke I know is 'what's green and stands in the corner.'"

"Hey! No stealing my jokes!" Rachel laughs again. He's not entirely sure why.

"That's the only joke I know."

"Really? Okay." She looks away from him. Out of the window. He watches her to see if she signals anyone. She doesn't, just stares out.

He waits a couple of seconds. Recalls another line. Tries it.

"Uncomfortable pause."

She snorts. Air forced out of her nose. "Yup."

"Sorry."

She looks back at him. "Hey, it's no problem."

"I'm just not – "

"Me neither."

He drinks. She sips. She is looking at him. He feels pinned by her. His stomach wrenches and twists for some reason he cannot fathom. He wonders what underwear she is wearing.

"What you thinking, Stan?"

His eyes widen. His cheeks burn. "N-Nothing. Just" the perfect line. "Just how pretty you are." Now smile confidently. He hopes he smiles.

"Aww, Stan." She looks at the table, then back at him. "You are so cute."

He swallows. "Thanks."

"I love your eyes. I've never seen eyes that color. And, do you work out? There's not an ounce of fat on you."

"Uh, work out? Not really." He's not fat because he doesn't eat all the poisons other people stuff in their faces.

Silence. The murmur of voices suddenly drowned out by the television.

"*– Kaczynski was arrested on charges of ten counts of transporting and using explosives, as well as the murders of three of his victims –*"

"Oh geez. They found him then." Rachel is watching the

screen over his shoulder. He twists in his chair to see, one hand still on his bottle. Safety first. A gaunt man in prison orange stares back at him. His beard is shot through with grey, his hair unkempt. He is replaced by a female reporter whose skin is too smooth and whose eyes are flat and dead. She is outside a police station in Montana, continuing to speak.

Rachel's voice over the television. "Hope he rots."

"Dies," Stan says. "They kill them in Montana." He turns back to her.

"Good. Ugh." She shudders. "What a sicko."

"Yeah. Imagine that." He hopes this is non-committal enough.

"I know, right? Mailing bombs to people. What the hell?"

Ah. The Unabomber. Stan recalls an article about him now. He wrote a book about what was wrong with society, but no one listened. Stan understands the frustration, but The Unabomber was stupid. He cut stems, not roots. Perhaps he had worked it out, discovered what Stan had learnt, but the realization had driven him… "Insane."

"Damn right insane." Rachel has put down her glass. It is empty though the ice slowly melts, replacing the alcohol with stale water. "He's a psychopath."

No. Possibly a sociopath. More likely just weak-willed and broken by the truth. Not a good topic to discuss with a spy for the company seeking to end the world.

He needs to steer the conversation away, last a little longer, then leave. No more drinks, certainly no food. Not when he can't be sure it isn't tainted. Just a little longer. Keep her talking. Learn more. Escape.

"Anyway," he says.

"Yeah, anyway." She leans back, visibly relaxes. Suspicious. "You hungry?"

Shit.

CHAPTER 12
MONDAY

His stomach flexes involuntarily. His throat opens. He removes his fingers from his mouth and painfully hot vomit splatters into the bowl. His throat is left raw. His body aches.

'Supper'. She had insisted. He had ordered the smallest salad he could. Ate little. Regurgitated even that.

He washes his hands with soap that smells of nothing but chemicals. Flicks his fingers above the cracked, stained sink. Droplets of water dash against the porcelain.

Fear ripples down his body, leaving gooseflesh in its wake. He is not used to being sick, not used to public washrooms. What if there's a camera in here, spying on him? He is trapped; there is no way out bar the way he came in. Rachel must have had another person in the bar, she must have informed her associates. Hot and cold panic narrows his vision. They can hear his thoughts. See him.

The outermost door to the washroom squeaks.

Stan backs away from the sink, back towards the cubicle. The inner door to the bathroom starts to open, a dark line widening as it is pushed.

He staggers into the cubicle, slams the door and locks it. His breathing is rapid. His ribs and stomach still ache. Sweat is beading on his forehead and lip. Someone walks in. Moves past the cubicle to the latrines. Stan is almost too scared to breathe. Flies are unzipped. Liquid rains against the plastic splashguard. Pauses. Restarts. Stops. Flies are zipped again. Footsteps, stopping opposite the cubicle door. Stan steps back, deeper into the corner of the toilet.

The rush of tap water. The trickle as the faucet is turned off. The noise from the bar sounds closer as first one door then another is opened. As they close, Stan is left alone. He hopes.

As quietly as he can, he slides the bolt across, the rasp of metal on metal painfully loud. He peers through a crack. Empty.

He brought his bag with him. She looked at him oddly, but he didn't care. He fishes in it now for his Walkman. Removes it and slides the headphones over his head. Presses play. Lowers the lid. Slumps on to it.

He remains there for a few minutes. The noise fills his ears, his skull. Fills his brain. He needs this, the white noise to block out everything else, to keep his thoughts his own. It's a temporary measure, but better than sitting there, his thoughts open. It's also the only way he knows to calm his nerves. His heart is hammering in his chest. He is shaking. It could have been no one, a random coincidence of time and space. Or, it could have been someone working with Rachel. An agent for the corporations. Or. Or.

Eventually, he turns off the Walkman. Sighs. Places it back in his bag. Unlocks the cubicle again. Leaves.

He tugs open the heavy wooden door and steps back into the bar. Ice Hockey commentary continues to dominate the room. A number of men sit in chairs facing the screen. The same group of card players are huddled in the back, not so far from the bathroom. There are some different shabbily dressed people. More men and women in suits. The talk is louder now, volume augmented by alcohol.

Stan winds his way back to the table. There is a fresh bottle of water on the table, open. Rachel has a full glass again. Her fourth. Her cheeks are flushed, but her eyes, the color of honey, are clear and focused.

He sits down, He craves a drink to wash the stench from his mouth and throat, but he cannot drink from the bottle in front of him.

They have passed another one hour and twenty-four minutes in banal conversation: Work, weather, her holidays and hobbies. He has made up two hobbies of his own: He collects beer mats and he skis. The first was easy to come by; his bottled water rests on a stained brown and red coaster. The second lie was a mistake, one he could never back up, but too late now. Rachel has already confirmed that she thought he skied, and is planning on them going skiing in the future.

She looks concerned. "Are you okay?"

He nods. He doesn't want to speak. Air will only mean he can taste the vomit again.

"Maybe they didn't wash the salad. You poor thing."

Bile rises. He forces himself not to think about it. "Yeah, maybe."

"What you wanna do now?"

A way out. Overdue, but he takes what he can get. Runs a hand over his stomach. "I should go."

A hint of something in her eyes. Disappointment? "Oh, yeah, totally."

Her look makes him feel uncomfortable. "Sorry."

She waves him off. "No, no. I mean, you're sick. You should totally go home."

He nods. Rises. He'll buy a bottle of water on the way.

Rachel stands. "Thank you for a great time, Stan. I'm so sorry about, y' know, the bad food." She takes her coat from the back of the chair, puts it on. Picks up her handbag. He slings his own bag over his shoulder.

He walks to the door. She follows. He opens it, walks through. It is dark outside, the streetlights tainting everything with a falsely warm orange glow. Remembering too late that he should open the door for her, he turns to Rachel.

"Well, bye."

She holds out her arms. Looks ridiculous. He stares at her.

She moves forward. Embraces him. "Thanks for a great time, Stan. We should do it again. Friday?"

He flinches, his shoulders hunching momentarily, almost pushing her away. He controls his survival instincts, but feels himself locked in place. Wills his body to move. Slowly raises his hands to her back. He notices how wide her back is. In keeping with her large frame. He taps her with his fingertips. Has to make her want to see him again. He pulls back from her. Forces another smile on his face. "Absolutely. No food next time!"

Rachel laughs. One hand strokes his arm. "Oh, Stan! Deal, no food!"

He holds the smile until he's worried he looks deranged. He rubs his stomach again. "I should go."

"Oh, of course. You get home ok? Get better. I'll see you at work tomorrow?"

Stan nods. Lies, "I hope so."

Rachel smiles warmly. "Bye then." She turns, waves once and walks away.

Stan gets his Walkman from his bag. Presses play and puts on his headphones. He takes one hour and fifty minutes to walk home. At each corner he looks over his shoulder. Rachel is not there. He isn't sure how this makes him feel.

* * * *

Home. Shuts himself in, twists the three locks. Walks to the windows in the dark and draws the curtains closed. Turns on the stereo. Returns to the front door and turns on the light switch. Light and sound fill the sparse chamber.

It feels like an age since he was last here, safe in his apartment. Slowly, he begins to relax, the tension of strangers, watchers and women draining from him, and he feels his muscles unwinding.

He should eat, but his abdominal muscles still ache and he doesn't want food. Instead he moves to the kitchen area and tugs open the fridge. The light is diffuse, filtered through row upon row of plastic mineral water bottles. Picking out one bottle, he unscrews the cap and drinks. He keeps the fridge turned down to make sure the water is near freezing. He enjoys the sensation of the cold liquid, the way it makes his tongue feel heavy, metallic.

Moving to the one armchair, he sinks into it. Breathes in. A long, slow inhalation. Holds it for a beat, then exhales. Repeats. His shoulders slump comfortably, his neck eases and he leans back, resting his head. His eyes close. The bottle nearly slips from his fingers, but he snaps back into consciousness. He screws the cap back on and places it on the floor before falling back again.

He remains there for some time.

His thoughts slowly, inexorably flow to the events of the evening. Rachel seemed so sincere, genuinely interested in him. Now, surrounded by walls and white noise, he examines how she made him feel, but cannot name the emotions. They are too new, too alien. He frowns. She makes him feel... somewhere between a god and a mouse.

He snorts. Ridiculous train of thought. He has far more important things to be worrying about. Rachel may well be trying to learn more about him, get closer to him, but she is working for someone.

He has everything he needs to find out who. He just needs the time and the place. He has an idea about both.

For now, however, he is exhausted and needs to sleep.

CHAPTER 13
TUESDAY

He wakes with a stiff neck. He takes in a deep breath and is suddenly aware of a foreign smell clinging to him. Rachel. The mixture of her perfume and skin. It is far from unpleasant, but its otherness makes him feel invaded, violated.

He peels himself from the armchair. He gathers the three unfinished plastic bottles of water from next to the chair and his bed. Removes his sweater and trousers and walks, slowly and uncomfortably, to the cramped bathroom.

White tiles on floor and walls. Everything clean. Washed once a week with bleach from Sweden.

The Shower is in one corner. Two panes of glass, two walls. Stan takes off his underwear and socks, pulls open one pane and steps inside. He slides the showerhead down its adjustable metal pole until it is level with his chest and shuts the door.

With a twist of his hand hot water hisses on to his skin.

He keeps his head up, chin towards the ceiling and ensures that no water can get into his mouth. He washes his body with unscented soap, starting with his shoulders, arms and armpits then working down his body. He finishes with his feet, including in between each toe.

Once his body is clean, he soaks his hair with one of the half-full bottles of mineral water. He uses the same unscented soap and rinses with the other two. As the last of the water trickles over his head, he picks up a small towel from its ring on the wall. He dries his hair with the small towel, his body with a larger towel. Like his mother used to.

Once dry, he shaves and then dresses in clean clothes and places the dirty laundry in the basket. Makes his lunch (cheese, bread) before leaving for work.

He walks to the office. Spends three hours fixing problems for idiots. Has lunch at his desk, ensuring his sandwich rests on the plastic bag in which he brought it. Folds the bag in half, then quarter, then into a small triangle, and puts it in to the front pocket of his backpack.

After lunch, he spends another three hours and fifty-four minutes moving between floors, helping suited chimps with facile computer issues. One in five of them acknowledges him. One in ten thanks him.

At 4.54pm, he opens a new email window. Types **Rachel E. Gundersson** in the address line. **Subject: Thanks**. He spends a few minutes agonizing over what to say. At 4.58pm he types as short a message as possible.

```
Thanks for last night. Maybe we can do it again.
Stan
```

He does not wait for a reply. At 5.00pm he shuts down,

picks up his bag and leaves.

Carpet, marble, rough mat and concrete. He takes one of his more usual routes back to the apartment. Dark clouds seem to sit on the tops of skyscrapers, darkening the afternoon. His skin prickles. Anticipating rain. As if in response, there is a muted flash above him. He looks up. Counts. Four seconds later and as thunder rumbles he feels panes of glass rattling. An hour later the first drops of rain, fat and heavy, burst on the sidewalk as Stan opens the door to his apartment.

10.17pm. The pregnant clouds continue to disgorge raindrops that are as much chemicals as they are water. They batter the window panes, a constant rattle to accompany Stan's movements around the room. He has finished his supper of rice and vegetables and washed up the plate and cutlery.

He gathers a black waterproof duffel bag from under the bed, places it on the mattress and fills it with the dirty clothes from his laundry basket. He gathers four quarters from the small pot of washed coins next to the sink and puts them in a pocket.

A cursory glance around his room to check for other dirty clothes. It is little more than habit. He does not leave clothes lying around. He zips up the bag, hefts it on to one shoulder and leaves the apartment. On the way out he takes his dark green waterproof from a hook by the door.

There are fourteen all-night laundromats within two hours of Stan's apartment. He visits thirteen of them on a weekly rotation. He varies the rotation each time. Tonight, it is the turn of *Biffco Cleaners*, situated on the outskirts of one of the smarter suburbs.

Stan discounts travelling by bus and subway immediately. Walking remains. It is raining steadily, but that doesn't bother him overly. He likes the rain. It drowns out sound, like natural white noise. And it drives people indoors. He pulls the waterproof's hood up and starts walking.

Once he reaches the financial district he is able to avoid a lot of the rain by clinging to the walls. The crenellations of the older buildings offer some shelter. The newer buildings, the glass and steel skyscrapers, do not. Capitalist phallic symbols adorning the city's skyline. Designed to intimidate and show off a company's wealth. Stan reflects that it is somewhere between narcissistic and desperate.

At night, this area of the city is quiet. With the offices shut, there is no reason to be here. White noise is turned down low, its constant comfort interspersed with the patter of rain on plastic.

The skyscrapers recede, replaced by increasingly smaller buildings. Obscene symbols of commerce are replaced by homes and local stores. The laundromat is between an Italian deli and a store called *Live it!*, whose glass front is hidden behind a metal security grille.

Biffco's sign is a feast of monochrome. Black and white and painfully trendy. The interior is that of a stylized 1950's diner, with checked floors, industrial washing machines where tables might be, and high-backed, booth-style faux leather seats forming an island in the middle.

Despite its obscene cool, it is always clean and the smell of the street, the uncleanness of humanity, doesn't penetrate the heavy glass door. It swings closed with the reassuring thump of a freezer door, sealing him in, and the filth of the streets out.

With the exception of a thin man with a shaven head and pink sweater vest, the laundromat is empty. The thin man sits limply at the back of the room, one foot dangling over a knee, shoulders sloped. His neck seems incapable of supporting his head.

The thin man looks up as Stan walks in and smiles. He sings, "Gooood evening," his voice is high-pitched, nasal, but has intrinsic warmth.

"Hi."

"Nice night, huh?"

"It's raining."

The limp man giggles girlishly. "I'll say!"

Stan isn't sure how to respond. He waits. The man's smile falters. Stan swallows and speaks. "I'd like to use a washer."

"Sure thing. You got change?"

"Yes."

The man waves dismissively. "Knock yourself out, hon."

Stan moves towards the back of the laundromat. The limp man looks like he is reading, but his eyes move from the page to Stan, then back again. Unsettled, Stan stops halfway between the door and the chair the limp man is sitting on.

He puts his bag on the red plastic leather diner-bench, unzips it and removes his clothes. All are dark. He does not own white clothes; they are too distinctive, too easily recognized. Much easier to blend into the crowd in dark, non-descript clothes. Nothing white or loud, nothing that will mean he is easily identified. His stomach clenches and he shivers. Not good thoughts. He pushes them away, imagines them as photographs of his childhood (sullen child on the grass, sullen child with unforgiving mother), replaces the faces with his unsettling thoughts, stylized images of his fears and then watches them as they burn and crinkle, the colors swirling as bubbles push through, blackening the thoughts beyond recognition. Blackening faces and memories.

A phone rings and Stan jumps.

The limp man picks it up after two rings. "Biffco Laundry." The phone is shaped like a hamburger with a shiny resin bun. The man speaks into the cheese. "Oh hi! How're you doing?"

Brief pause.

"Oh no! No way? Really?" The discussion continues as the man slinks into the chair.

Stan pushes his bundle of clothes into the large washer, forcing the mound of dark fabrics through the small hole. All the while, the limp man is talking, pausing, talking.

"I told that bitch, I told him, I said 'Bruce, that boy will tear your heart out,' and what happened?"

Pause.

"I know, I know! I mean, I don't want to say I told you so, but **fzzzzzzzz** –" White noise drowns out all other sounds as Stan's thumb rolls over the volume wheel.

He pulls a small bottle of concentrated detergent (from Sweden, like all his cleaning products) from his bag, unscrews the lid and pours a cap full into the right tray. Closes the machine door, fishes a quarter from his pocket and drops it into the washer. Twists the dial and pushes 'start', then sits down to wait.

The static drowns out sound completely, insulating him. The rain forms rivulets down the windowpanes, while the limp man continues to gesticulate languidly from his chair.

Stan can feel the fake leather squeaking under him when he moves. He imagines the noise, how loud and intrusive it is. The potential future embarrassment locks him in place. Gingerly, he pushes his backside off the seat and shuffles his body backwards. He leans his head against the high backrest and watches the machine fill. He turns down the volume on his Walkman again, and watches his clothes flatten as they absorb water, moving around the drum to the soothing swish and heave of the washing machine.

Stan watches the hypnotic motions of the laundry. The warm, clean smell of detergent fills his nose and the comforting insulating sounds of the washer and static fill his ears. His mind turns to Cassandra and his plans to prevent the advent of the apocalypse. It has been a long time, and it seems unavoidable that soon Project Cassandra will be put into motion, and it will be too late. He needs to find out which company is researching it, who is at the head of the serpent. Someone is responsible for the project's creation, someone is driving it. If Stan can find that person and stop them, remove that keystone, the project should collapse. He hopes.

Then there's Friday. The day when he finally learns what he needs to know. He hopes. For all his efforts, all his planning, everything comes down to hope. He snorts quietly to himself. This reliance on luck amuses him even as it frustrates him. So much hinges on the Sodium Pentothal working, on him being able to find the designer of the project, and being able to stop him from continuing with it.

The washer slows. The clothes, wet and dark, sit at the bottom of the drum. Stan turns up the volume on his Walkman again, leaves the bench and opens the machine door. Removes the bundle of damp clothes and moves around the fake leather seats to the row of dryers. He lifts the lid with one hand, and tips the clothes in. Closes the lid. Inserts another quarter. He retrieves his bag and detergent and sits facing the dryer.

The limp man is off the phone. His head hangs over a copy of a celebrity gossip magazine. Stan leans back. Comes as close to relaxing as he can in a public place.

Time passes, the minutes sliding by as Stan lets his mind fill with static. He enters a near-trance. His mind begins to wander from thought to thought, linked by abstracts. Rachel drinking a Cassandra beer, then playing ice hockey with him as he walks a snow-capped mountain, the snow becoming ash, filling his vision with warm, comforting darkness.

The buzz of the dryer barely cuts through the white noise, but it is enough to draw him from his near-sleep. He blinks, squeezing his eyelids closed and then forcing them wide. Takes a deep breath.

The limp man's mouth is moving. He is waving a thin, weedy hand. Stan pulls out one headphone.

"Your laundry's dry, hon." The limp man smiles at him.

"Uh, thanks." Stan stands and pulls out the laundry. He sifts through it. Underwear and socks go straight into the duffel bag. Trousers he folds before placing them on top of the underwear. Eventually, only tops remain in the pile. T-shirts and sweaters that can go in the dryer he lies flat on the seat, before awkwardly folding them and then gently placing them in the bag. Work shirts he buttons up, ensuring the collars are neat. He shakes out the creases and then folds the sleeves behind the body of the shirt, halves it and stores them in the top.

"Sure you don't want to use the folding table?" The limp man is watching Stan over the top of his magazine.

Stan doesn't respond. Starts to zip up the bag.

"Oh darling, you really shouldn't just leave them like that." He's moving around the table, a near-boneless saunter towards Stan. "Here, let me help." His thin wrist and too hairy arm reach around Stan and pluck up a t-shirt. A deft twist and Stan's painstaking folding is undone.

"Uh –" Stan tries to think of something to say. Fails.

The limp man moves to the folding table. Flicks the t-shirt, twists his hands and guides the garment to the Formica.

Stan moves closer. His fists flex with nervous tension. Wants to snatch his shirt back, thrust the man away, but he doesn't know if he can.

A few more quick motions and the limp man presents an immaculately folded t-shirt. "Now, isn't that better?" His smile is genuine. It makes Stan feel suddenly uncomfortable.

He snatches the top. Stuffs it in to his bag.

"Hey now?"

Stan ignores him and hurries from the laundromat.

"You're welcome!" The limp man's half-shriek chases him out of the glass door, into the dark and the rain.

CHAPTER 14
WEDNESDAY

A white screen. There is light behind it, pale and diffuse. He is both behind the screen and watching it. He watches himself move, jerkily, arms and legs swiveling on pinpoint axes. A strange, two-dimensional caricature of himself.

Another flat shadow shuffles into the light. A woman. Her limbs have arabesques of light swirling through them. She moves toward him, then away. One hand on her brow, the other pushed out, towards Stan's shadow.

Then, suddenly, she is pressed against him. Their shadows merging through the screen. He can neither see nor feel where she ends and he begins. His arms rise in small twitches, seeming to embrace her.

The woman turns, becoming a thin line of black in the light. When she turns back, her shadow is not that of a woman, but a dragon, rent through with jagged lightning slashes. He watches her menace his shadow, feels the heat of her breath.

His shadow, a brave looking warrior, draws a flat paper sword and cuts the dragon, who cries out and falls away.

But, Stan cannot celebrate the victory he sees and experiences. Even as the dragon disappears beneath the screen, More shadow puppets dive on to the screen. Long and thin, pointed. Bombs and missiles and strafing bullets.

They dive and fly overhead, as the white light becomes red, they fill more and more of the screen before Stan. Bombs explode and missiles shriek as they crush the earth, closer and closer, and Stan knows he will be destroyed, crushed to nothing. He raises his arms, and silently screams...

Screams fill his ears, horribly loud. His own terror deafens him. He is clutching his head. Shaking. Sweating. He can't breathe. It's come. The end of the world. He can't move his legs. Dear God, his legs!

He thrashes and struggles. Finally, the sheets relinquish their hold. He can move again. He runs to the window and pulls back a curtain.

The world is dark, serene. Night interrupted only by pools of orange street light. He releases the breath he didn't know he was holding. He still has time. He crawls back to bed and quickly makes barely comprehensible notes filled with half-formed phrases of panic. That done, he falls asleep.

His alarm wakes him again. His rises on to his elbows and winces. His head throbs. Tiredness and apprehension. He wipes the sleep-grit from his eyes and pulls himself out of bed. Cleans and dresses, readies himself for work.

Work is dull and listless. On the way home he buys three different newspapers. Watches his program, creates questions to answers the host provides. Reads the papers in bed. Nothing very interesting: both The Tiresias Corporation and Delphic Electronics report continuing profits, both claim to be working on a next generation program that will revolutionize computing and the applications of computers. This is hardly news. Neither company has named their program, but he is certain that one of them is working on Project Cassandra. Of course they wouldn't name it; that would only help him. But, despite all their efforts, they've made a mistake. They gave him a way of learning the truth and locating the creator.

Rachel.

The dangerous, beautiful, oddly delightful Rachel.

He's exhausted other avenues – he's tried papers, libraries, even the World Wide Web – but any information about Cassandra is hidden within labyrinthine systems behind firewalls that Stan just cannot begin to fathom. He's good, but he has neither the knowledge nor the skill to begin breaking in to systems protected by the government. And, even if he could, what if they could follow his efforts back to his apartment? All his hard work to remain more or less anonymous, to remain a small, pointless, worthless speck, will have been for nothing.

No, much better to wait. Friday is soon. If Rachel agrees to the 'date' he can ask her all he needs to know. He will be so much closer to saving the world. Saving the world. The stupid, petty world. His hatred of the world, and his desperate need to save it, war within him as he drifts off.

* * * *

His alarm wakes him from a dreamless sleep. Slowly he realizes it is Thursday, 7.01am. Another day at work.

His walk takes 52 minutes. His route slightly circuitous but his pace quicker than usual. An urge to check his mail, to see if Rachel has replied. As he walks, his headphones in, Stan tries to justify his desire. It is important to have as much notice of any potential meeting as possible. He needs to know if he can meet her at all or if he has to try something else. Other self-delusions accompany him through the revolving door and across the squeaky marble.

His arm of the swastika is quiet this morning. He turns on the monitor before he has sat down and checks his internal emails.

```
Carter.P.Burke        Mouse broken            08.47
Rebecca.X.Demchenko   Lost all Files!         08.52
Rachel E. Gundersson  Re: Thanks              08.58
<Internal Memo>       Ensure you're Secure!   09.00
Ben.A.Gorman          Software Assistance     09.01
```

Moves his cursor over Rachel's email and opens it.

```
Re: Thanks
A walk in the park Friday would be great! Maybe a
drink first in D'Amico's again? It can be our new
local!!!

Rx
```

He winces and closes the email. The repeated exclamation marks upset him. He feels like they are flash-bangs at the end of the sentence, hurting his eyes.

Nevertheless, this is good news. He can do what needs to be done on Friday. The thought causes his stomach to clench, a strange cold heaviness fill his gut. Doubts and fear. His breath catches and he coughs gently. He feels ridiculous. He's a computer geek, not a hero. How can he trick a spy, capture her, interrogate her and then hunt down and stop a real-life Blofeld?

But, there is no one else. Or at least, no one that he knows. No one he can rely on to save the world. He was chosen, guided by some force. It's his destiny. He squares his shoulders and clicks 'reply' from the inbox page. He is not quite ready to face the exclamation marks again.

```
Re: Thanks
That's good. I will see you at 5.00pm in the
foyer.
Stan
```

That done, he focuses on drudgery. Travels the floors, fixing problems. He is distracted, unable to concentrate on what anyone says while he is there. They have already emailed him the problem, he already knows the solution or, if he doesn't know already, then talking to any of these idiots is unlikely to help.

`Mouse broken` – cable not connected properly. `Lost all Files!` – lost one file, by saving it in a temp folder, rather than on the hard drive. `Software Assistance` – moron had deleted the shortcut to his word-processing program. He takes his time with all of these problems. He is no rush to return to his desk and gather more tasks. That's not the corporate way. Take your time, drag it out. It's the unwritten code of the small-cog-employee. Don't be too efficient, don't show anyone up or mark yourself out as exceptional.

After lunch, he has six more requests for assistance. He stays late to ensure that all problems are solved, before taking his bag and heading home. He crosses the street and takes an unusual three-sides-of-a-square route home. He keeps his head down and studies the concrete as he walks.

The evening is quiet, the radio is turned down low, but there are no sounds from the street to intrude, and the static is loud enough to keep him safe and isolated, his thoughts hidden away behind walls of sound. The only noise is that of his fingers on keys, a strange plastic tapping.

Stan's face is lit by the monitor, painting his skin a blue-white. His searching the World Wide Web this evening has yielded some potentially vital information and he is trying to find out more. An internal memo that was then cut/pasted on to some 'future technologies' discussion board. Lots of things were cut or blanked out, but the content of the memo is enough to have Stan both excited and terrified.

```
All,

It is with great pleasure that I announce
the arrival of Nathan Schultz to the
████████ team. Nathan will be working
with me on bringing my vision of PC to
life, are we're hoping to present it to
████████████ and his advisors in the
next few weeks.

Nathan comes to us from a freelance
background in technology research and has
been instrumental in numerous
developments in the fields of Artificial
Intelligence, Remote Visibility and
Command packages and of course
probability data resolution and
manipulation.

As you all know, we're pinning a great
deal on PC. However, we're also extremely
optimistic that this software will mark a
new era, both for The Tiresias
Corporation and for ████████████,
```

following the recent .

Kind regards,
Damien Veidt
CEO

Following this post on the discussion boards are three pages of various technical wizards and computer wonderkids discussing what Nathan Schultz one-time super-hacker and thorn in the side of governments and mega-corporations, was doing working for The Tiresias Corporation, and what he was working on. New encryptions to defeat even the near-mythical hackers of the decade? Perhaps tracing programs? Or, was it following on from his more legitimate freelance work, building a new AI or some sort of remote dial-in package? There was no shortage of theories.

And they are all wrong. Whatever Schultz and Veidt are working on, it was weapons-related. Designed to wreak ruin. Veidt has been the creative force behind every single great technical leap forward for The Tiresias Corporation since he took over in the mid-eighties. He's a genius. And, according to the comments on the 'Web, so is Schultz. It sounds like a powerful combination.

However, further searching, following links, tracking various people who have commented on things others said Schultz said, following an electronic paper trail, leads Stan to discover that Schultz has been drafted in to create coding and handle the technical development, rather than provide any ideas or creative input. He's a minion. A skilled builder of Veidt's designs.

Stan spends a further 21 minutes scouring the World

Wide Web for more information, before returning to the original Web site where he found the internal memorandum. The memo has vanished, as have all the comments. Indeed, the Web site is blank, except for a single line:

This Web site is experiencing technical difficulties

CHAPTER 15
FRIDAY

At 6.00am, he gets out of bed. He has barely slept. Minutes here and there. He is exhausted, but his stomach churns constantly, nervous energy that will grant him no rest.

When he is cleaned and dressed, he considers breakfast, but cannot eat. Instead, he moves about the apartment in the pre-dawn shadows and gathers the things he needs: gloves, pack of cable ties, syringes and needles, and the small vial of Sodium Pentothal. He still needs to buy something he can tie with, but he can acquire that on the way to work. In the movies they use belts, but he's not sure where he could get one on the way to work, and he is not happy touching something that is most likely riddled with mind-altering chemicals and strange cow-steroids.

He wraps the needles, syringe and vial in a sock. Places the sock in one of the gloves. The ties in another. Places everything in an old brown grocery bag and stashes it in the bottom of his backpack.

At 8.09am he stops at a mini-mart not too close to the office and purchases a roll of Saran Wrap, then continues to work.

It is still light at 5.00pm. Stan stands in the foyer, an inkblot of uncomfortable darkness in the corner of the clinical white marble hall. It is 5.02pm when the door across the foyer opens and Rachel walks through. She is dressed smartly in a blue blouse, though the fabric is stretched slightly. Her blond hair reflects the sun as it shines through the glass of the building.

"Hey there!" Her smile is attractively toothy. Her lips are an unnatural bright pink. Stan has never noticed these details about someone before. Her honey-colored eyes are bright and shining. She looks happy. It puts him on edge. He feels his eyes narrow.

"Hi."

"It's good to see you again," she continues to smile, her hands on her handbag strap.

His responding smile is brief at best. "Shall we go?"

"Sure! D'Amico's again first, then a nice walk in the park?"

He says nothing. He wants to smile confidently. He can't. His heart is in his throat. He cannot swallow properly.

Rachel loops one arm in his as they walk. Her body grazes his, but somehow does not disrupt his walking. This synergy sends strange pulses through him. They are not unpleasant, but they are distracting.

Already she is talking.

" —believe the week I've had. First there was –"

He tunes her out. Her voice is like impotent radio static. It has no power to protect or insulate, but it is a monotony that he can accept without complaint. However, he must guard his thoughts. He is not safe without white noise.

"—your week?"

He's on. Time for him to lie and fake. He can do this. He can do this. "My week was the same as usual. Computer problems."

"Oh I hear that!" Her squeaky laugh. He likes it, but it makes him nervous. Like it is a sign or codeword of some kind. He glances around, but no one seems to be paying them attention. Nevertheless, he is on edge.

It is three blocks to D'Amico's. During the journey, Stan listens to every word Rachel says and repeats it mentally. An attempt to create an internal wall of sound.

"So I told him I simply wasn't going to accept those figures for the first quarter and Bob – You know Bob Travers, up on third – he totally agreed with me so –"

Stan still doesn't know Bob Travers. He'll never know Bob Travers. He's not even sure that the company owns the third floor.

" – which reminds me, we're going to need your help with pulling some data at some point, so we'll be working together!" She grins at him. He shivers with dread and something else all at once.

"Um. OK," Stan avoids eye contact.

D'Amico's red, white and green awning casts the wooden tables and chairs into shadow. Several tables are already occupied by business men and women enjoying an early evening drink to start the weekend.

Inside, electric lighting replaces the weak, evening sunlight. There is one table unoccupied near the front of the bar, by one of the large windows. Stan tries to ignore it and move towards the bar. The noise of the television wars with the sound of Italian opera.

"There's a table by the window."

Stan cringes. "Oh, yes. So there is." He does not want to sit by a window, in plain sight, easily observed.

"Lucky, huh? It's packed in here. You grab the table, I'll get the drinks. What would you like?"

Half a dozen scenarios flash through his head: various drugs dropped into a bottle of water, dissolving in seconds. He drinks. He passes out. Wakes up in a metal room and is tortured for information.

"I'll get the drinks." What did she have before? It was initials. "Would you like a gee and tee?"

"Aw, aren't you a gentleman. That'd be great." She winks at him. He is not sure what that means.

The same bored-looking, fat, Italian Elvis is behind the bar. He is staring at the small television screen in the corner of the room with cold, reptilian eyes. Stan reaches the bar. The smell of alcohol that has permeated the wood of the bar over the years makes his nose twitch.

"Wad can I ged ya?" The bartender doesn't look at Stan.

"A bottle of San Nicolo still water and a gee and tee."

"Sure," he reaches for two glasses without taking his eyes from the screen and places them on the bar. Fumbles under the bad and shovels some ice into them. Drags his eyes from the screen long enough to pour a measure of gin into one glass, then tops it up with tonic water. Finally, reaches for a bottle of water from a glass-fronted fridge. He grasps the lid of the bottle and Stan reaches out reflexively.

"Don't open it."

The fat Italian Elvis impersonator shrugs, but leaves the

lid on. "Thad'll be nine-fifty."

Stan hands over a ten-dollar bill. He doesn't wait for the dirty change, but awkwardly carries two glasses and a bottle to the table. Rachel watches him as he walks over. He is not sure what she is thinking. Makes him nervous.

"Thanks!" She takes a long sip. "Mmm, I so need this. What a week!"

Stan unscrews the cap. Eschews the glass and drinks straight from the bottle. He takes his time. He has nothing to say, and is too nervous to say anything anyway.

"So, you were saying: How was your week?"

He puts down the bottle. Slowly swallows. Rachel waits. Her smile suggests she finds his delay amusing. He realizes he can't escape with silence. "Yeah. You know."

"Same shit, different day, huh?" She continues to smile over her glass as she sips. "And what else is going on?"

She knows something. They've found him. Know he is the one searching for them. He should never have agreed to meet this woman. Mouth drying, he drinks.

His mind races. He has not prepared for this meeting. "Not much. Work mostly. Jeopardy."

Rachel laughs. Reaches over and touches his arm lightly. "Oh Stan, you are *so* funny! I'd forgotten you love that show! You know, I watched it this week. It's actually kinda cool. I'm not so good at it though. I could do the easy ones, you know 'Who is Abraham Lincoln?', but 'Who is Albert Einstein?' You're kidding me! How was I supposed to work that out?"

Stan snorts. Almost laughs. Then catches himself. This is an act. She is not endearingly stupid and in awe of his genius. She's trying to manipulate him. Lull him. He will not be caught.

"It's not that hard really," Stan thinks quickly. "You're really smart. It just takes practice."

"Aww, you're so sweet."

Forced smile. Hopes it looks genuine. It probably doesn't. "Another drink?"

"Sure, but let me get this." Rachel reaches into her purse for her wallet. "You want another water? Or maybe something stronger?"

"Oh, no. I'm fine with this one for now, thanks."

"If you're sure..." she rises and moves to the bar. Stan could watch her from his position next to the window, but he doesn't want to draw attention to himself by staring to one side. He focuses on the bottle, his thumb drawing fat lines through the condensation, wiping away small droplets of water.

Rachel returns. She places her glass on the table. Her drink is pink and cloudy. There is a small paper umbrella sticking out of it, next to a ridiculous curly straw. He cannot help but recoil from its ostentation.

She laughs. "You look horrified! It's only a cocktail. I figure it's Friday, so why not?"

Stan cannot tear his eyes away from it. He sees now that the pink is slowly separating into pink and orange, two mixed liquids unmixing. Like oil and water.

With a flick of her wrist, the straw swirls around the glass, throwing the colors together, blending them back into pepto-pink. She sucks. Stan watches the pink glide up the straw, loop-the-loop through the plastic and disappear in to her mouth. Her lips are pursed. Full and dark. His stomach twists. As does something else.

Her lips release the straw. The alcohol sinks back down the straw. He looks up again. Her eyes are twinkling as they focus on him. Something in them seems soft, unfocused.

"I didn't have lunch, so to be honest I probably shouldn't be drinking this."

Why is she telling him this? Some sort of lure? A ploy to set him at ease, perhaps. He will not be drawn in.

He has no idea how to continue. He opts for crass, tactless flirtation. Play her game. "I'm sure you can handle a couple. Besides, I won't take advantage of you," Stan doesn't know how to wink, or he would. One side of his mouth curls up. He hopes it looks flirtatious and not or lascivious.

Rachel sips on the cocktail. Pauses. "Shame," she says. Unlike Stan, she can wink.

CHAPTER 16
FRIDAY

Rachel finishes her second cocktail. Stan has finished his bottle of water. A shot glass of dark brown alcohol stands untouched on the table. He wants to try it, but he's scared. It might give him a shot of courage. It might make him lose control. And, of course, there could be anything in it.

Nevertheless, he finds the unknown tempting tonight. Not tempting enough, but tempting. The closest he can come to drinking it is moving the glass on the table between one finger and thumb. Even with the din of the bar, he can hear the glass grating against the wood.

Rachel is talking. Alcohol has somehow made her breathe less between sentences. " – and so that's why they divorced, but like I said I was only nine. They still don't get on too well, but they make an effort when they need to, y'know? And I'm totally cool with it –"

If the story were true, she'd be lying about being cool. As it is, Stan is reasonably certain that it's fabricated. Too clichéd. If it was true, then Rachel is more fucked up than an industrial spy should be.

She continues to talk. He looks into her eyes. Through them. She becomes a droning blur. He glances to one side. The outside world has grown darker. The light in D'Amico's fills the window panes.

He cuts her off. He's not sure what she's talking about. "Would you like another drink? Or, maybe a walk? A little bit of fresh air?"

Her smile is slow, conspiratorial. "Sure, let's go for a walk. It's a nice night for it."

They stand and leave D'Amico's. The night is warm and dry, but noisy. The traffic, the people, the music wafting from bars. The sounds, cacophonous and jarring, stab into Stan's ears. He can almost feel coded messages and governmental impulses layered through every decibel.

Rachel leans against him, her arm wrapped around one of his. A subconscious need for support. Alcohol has made her unsure on her feet.

The park is a short walk. He'd like to take a circuitous route. Check over his shoulder, look for anyone who might be paying them undue attention. However, the streets in this part of the city are busy, workers and weekenders mingling as they walk to or from the numerous bars and offices in the area. No one drinks on the street. Not now. The mayor of the city has cracked down on drinking in public. Show a bottle on the street, the police will arrest you. First strike.

Nevertheless, the mood is already buoyant. It makes Stan twitchy. People lurch out of shadows, or storm towards him talking loudly. A few men already weave and stagger, threatening to collide with him. He feels his entire body tensing. A primordial readiness for fight or flight.

Rachel seems to have no such worries. Like so many, she is blithely unaware of the world around her. She moves between people easily despite her size, her own unsteady steps somehow in rhythm with the pace of everyone else. Somehow, although leaning on him, Rachel guides him. He allows himself to dragged along, his own steps faltering. Unsure.

The streets open out, the roads becoming larger as they near the large park around which so much of the city is anchored. It becomes easier to walk, their path less obstructed. Soon, there is just one wide street between Stan and the orange-lit park.

As he and Rachel wait at a pedestrian crossing, she rests her head on his shoulder. Involuntary he shrugs and she stands upright.

"Sorry," she says, quickly.

"No. Sorry. I, um. Just, we can cross."

The white light flashes as he guides her across the asphalt and paint. On the far side, the park waits, shadows and yellow light, grass the color of flames. Quiet and almost-solitude. Fire and silence.

The park is an expansive open space, riddled with paths and entrances. They reach the sidewalk and cross it to one of these paths. Rachel's arm is still wrapped around Stan's. He is in danger of becoming used to the feeling.

The path meanders through the grass. Trees line some walkways in military order, while in other areas there is no human design. The park isn't particularly busy, though this close to the business district it is busier than Stan would like, so he leads Rachel deeper in, further from the noise of traffic, from the potential of passersby.

"It really is a lovely night," Rachel sighs. "This was a great idea, Stan. You can spend so much time in the city and sort of forget that there are these big, beautiful, quiet places where you can just wander. Sorta…" Stan glances at her. She is searching for the right word.

"Get lost?" he offers.

"Exactly. You can lose yourself."

For some reason, she extricates her arm from his. "So, what do you want to do now?"

Shit. "I figured we'd just walk around. Get away from all the people, you know?" Think of something innocent and tacky to say. "Maybe sit and look at the stars." Perfect. Even though it's impossible to see stars through the light pollution the millions of ignorant ants in this city spew into the atmosphere. Even in the park there are street-lamps (bad imitations of old-fashioned gas lamps) to further obscure the night sky.

"Got somewhere in mind?"

"Not really. We'll know when we find it."

She smiles. It seems so genuine. Then she glances over her shoulder.

Stan is immediately on guard. He looks back as well. There is a man in a suit with an umbrella perhaps fifty paces behind them. He is walking briskly in their direction, briefly lit up in the glow of one of the park's streetlights. Then hidden by darkness.

Is he in league with Rachel? Are they intending on kidnapping him? He feels cold. Panicked.

He balls up his fists but keeps walking. Rachel has not slowed her steps. She does not seem to be paying attention to the man behind them. Studious ignorance?

She moves closer to him. One arm reaches for him. He avoids her grasp. Entering a circle of white light, Stan drops to one knee.

"You ok?"

"Yeah, shoelace. One moment."

'Oh. Sure." She sounds upset.

He fiddles with his laces, head down, looking behind him as much as he can. The man continues to walk briskly towards them. Umbrella in one hand, briefcase in another. He is twenty paces behind them.

Ten.

Stan rises to his feet. His hands are curled into fists again.

"Done?" She is smiling.

Stan nods. "Done." He tries to smile back.

Five.

He can hear the man's shoes on the path. Stan spins to face him. He has no idea what he can or will do, but he's determined to fight.

The man looks surprised, nervous. He takes as wide a berth as he can without walking on the grass. His leather shoes shine in the lamplight as he almost scampers past. He doesn't speak.

"Whoa, Stan, you ok?"

"He surprised me, that's all."

"Haha, can't be too careful these days, huh?"

Stan doesn't reply. He lets out a held breath.

Rachel sidles closer to him. "Let's keep walking. It's a lovely night."

They walk. Light to dark to light. It is quiet, except for occasional couples walking other paths.

"Let's go that way," Rachel points ahead.

Stan feels her other hand reaching for his. The idea terrifies him, but he lets her hand bind his. He shudders. Being tied to her, her fingers laced with his. The pressure on his knuckles. The germs. It makes him queasy.

She is blissfully unaware. Or pointedly ignoring his discomfort. Suddenly, Stan is not in control of the situation. Again, the all-too-familiar feeling of disquiet swells up from his gut.

He needs to regain some sort of composure. He needs to guide her somewhere quiet. Somewhere –

The path rises steeply. A bridge. Rachel pulls him on to it. She leans against the wall. He looks over. The bridge is old, ivy-covered stone. Beneath is water, dark and slow.

"Wow. Isn't this beautiful? So romantic!"

Stan spies another couple walking towards the bridge from the other way. This place is probably a regular nightspot for young couples. He imagines the queue of couples, each standing some way apart from each other, waiting their turn on the romantic bridge. He snorts.

"What? Are you laughing at me?" Rachel pulls him toward her. He doesn't resist. He can't afford to. He is pressed against her body. She is warm and soft.

"What's so funny, Stan?" her voice is low. "Laughing at

my romantic side?"

"N-no. No. Just laughing." Fuck. He knows he sounds lame. Not good. He needs to recover, but her hands have let go of his and slipped around his waist. He is trapped against her. Terrified.

He doesn't know where to put his hands. Places them on the wall either side of her. Rachel's hands are a slight but insistent tugging on him. Her head is moving closer, sidling towards him like a snake. Something about her smile is different. Stan doesn't know a word for it.

Rachel is looking at him. Staring into his eyes. "You really do have beautiful eyes, Stan. So… kind."

Her face is so close to his he can feel her breath on his face. Sweet, with the tang of alcohol. His head turns away slightly, involuntarily. Rachel's lips press against his cheek. He freezes. She moves slightly and her mouth is pressed against his. It is slightly sticky from her lipstick.

He doesn't know what to do. His mind is whirling. He is being kissed. She could be poisoning him. She could be marking him out to someone. He is being kissed.

Her tongue, her *tongue*, pushes against his mouth. Shocked, his lips offer little resistance. It is in his mouth, only briefly. A moment. Soft, wet and warm. He is repulsed. The invasive intimacy is too much. He will need to wash his mouth out with bleach. He pulls back. His hands leave the wall. He tries to be gentle as he moves Rachel from his body.

She pouts. "What's wrong?"

"Nothing," he lies. He wants to scream. "Just…" he looks to one side. "There are people coming. I think maybe they want their turn."

"Oh, ohh. Sure. Well, we can keep walking for a bit. I'm sure there are some other nice places." One finger runs down his chest.

He smiles. Genuine relief. He's regaining some measure of control. He takes her hand (he needs to wash his hands in bleach as well, as soon as he can) and leads her off the bridge.

Off to one side he can see a squat building. Public bathrooms. He leads Rachel in that direction.

She pulls him back a little and kisses him again. He purses his lips and tries to kiss back without seeming too awkward.

They walk side by side. He is a little taller and wraps one arm around her shoulders. She leans into his chest. They walk, slowly, along the wide, flat path.

As nonchalantly as he can manage, Stan walks near the bathrooms. He glances over his shoulder. He can just make out another couple embracing on the bridge. There is no one else that he can see.

They near the bathroom entrance. A high, narrow corridor running alongside the building. Stan's arm is still around Rachel's shoulders. He looks down at her. She looks up. They smile at one another.

He slaps his free hand over her mouth. His arm wraps tightly around her throat. He drags her backwards the few feet into the concrete corridor. She squeals and claws at his face and arms. He jerks his head back out of harm's way and turns into the bathroom.

She continues to fight. He is not strong enough to control her for long. Her heels scrabble on the concrete floor. The lights flicker and blink.

Sudden pain as Rachel bites the flesh of his palm. He

snarls and whips his hand away. Rachel draws breath to scream. He balls his injured hand into a fist. With one arm still around her throat, he flings his fist at the side of her head. Her knees buckle.

Unconscious, she is too heavy. He lowers her to the ground as best he can.

The heavy metal door to the bathroom is pinned back against the inside wall by a hook through a hole affixed to the concrete. Stan unhooks the door. It moves with a deep rumbling as it scuffs the floor. Closes with a flat metallic bang.

CHAPTER 17
FRIDAY

The strip-light hums, a convergence of sound and light just above his head. He breathes deeply, lungfuls of bleach and urine. Lets the hum fill his ears, drowning out his thoughts as the not-bright-enough neon tube flickers, light in its death throes.

His hands shake as he clutches the small vial. He pierces the foil, slides the needle inside, and pulls gently. Withdraws the point, squeezes. A tear glides along the smooth, unblemished metal.

He's nervous, excited. He hasn't done this before, but he's studied Trainspotting and Pulp Fiction. He doesn't have a belt. He uses the Saran Wrap, twisted into a tight, plastic cord. He rests the syringe on a metallic paper dispenser defaced by blue pen: *Frankie Fucked Here*. He wraps the Saran Wrap around and around. He should have studied knots.

Stan steadies himself. He needs to get this right first time or he'll lose his nerve. His thumb caresses the skin below the Saran Wrap until he sees purple snaking, pulsing. The beating wars with the stuttering of the strip-light. He blinks, closes his eyes, focuses. Places the needle and applies pressure. It slips through skin and he feels the slightest resistance as he enters the vein. He pauses, remembering the image of blood swirling in fluid. He pushes, slowly, gently.

Her honey-colored eyes widen. She whines through the gag.

"I'm sorry. But, I have to know what you know. I need to stop it." He'd tell her if he thought she'd believe him. But she wouldn't, so he swallows the words and hopes his eyes convey apology. He has no choice.

The hum continues, keeping them safe as he lets the Sodium Pentothal take effect.

* * * *

Rachel has lapsed into a semi-conscious state. She moans quietly on the toilet, as if having a bad dream. Her hands are tied with cable ties. He has removed her high heels; their sharpness scares him. Her ankles are also tied.

She begins to raise her head. Her moans become a little louder.

"Shh, be quiet please." Stan removes the Saran-Wrap gag. Rachel's head lolls around on her shoulders. Seems drunk more than anything.

"Stan, what's going on? Hey I can't move my arms properly did you know I can'tmovemyarmsproperly?" The words slur together, her mouth slack.

"Hey Rachel," he tries to sound friendly. His heart is

beating hard. The strip-light flickers above them. Its staccato flashes like neon lightning. "Can you help me figure some things out?"

"Shure Stan Icandothat."

"Great. So, who are you working for, really?"

"That'sh a silly question – I work with you, Shtan." Her lids cover her eyes as she speaks.

"No, you work for the Tiresias Corporation. You're working for the government, trying to find out about me, aren't you." He is struggling to keep the edge out of his voice.

"No, Shtan. Whatareyoutalking'bout?"

"You know what I'm talking about."

"No, I don'. Why can't I move my arms, Shtan? Shtan, I'm a little scared." Her voice is quiet, small.

Stan squats in front of her. He does his best to smile reassuringly. "Hey, it's ok. We're just playing a game."

Rachel calms. "Ohhh, a game? 'Slike roleplay or summing?"

He doesn't know what roleplay is. "Yes, just like that."

"Have I been a bad girrrl?" Despite slurring, she seems to purr the last word, as if being bad were a good thing.

"Yes, you have. So now you need to tell me about Tiresias and Project Cassandra."

"I can't, Shtan," she looks sad briefly. Then giggles. "I guesh you'll have to punishme!"

Clearly that tack is not one he wants to follow. "Rachel, you like me, don't you?"

She smiles. A drunken leer that conveys exactly how she feels about him. He shudders.

"Well, if you like me, you'll want to help me. I really need you to tell me what you have found out about me."

"You like shkiin' and beermats. You cute. You a bit weird, but I like that."

"And what have you told your bosses about me? Have you told Veidt?"

"Who'sthat? I've told my bosses you are clean as a whistle. No personal calls. You're a model employee. So model I'm suspicious."

"Suspicious? Of what?"

"Shomeone that clean? Gotta besomedirt." Did she just wink?

"Come on, Rachel. Tell me the truth. Why did the Tiresias Corporation set you on me?"

She shakes her head.

"Don't shake your head. Tell me. Why did they send you? What do they know?"

"Nothing, Shtan. I don't know. I couldn't say." She is starting to sound a little upset, a little clearer. "My arms, Shtan. I can't move my arms." Her bare feet push against the cracked tiles. "Help me, Stan. Please?" Her eyes are wide, pleading.

Her movements are weak but increasingly frantic. The Saran Wrap is not strong enough to hold her, even with the shitty knots he's managed to tie.

Stan straightens. The Sodium Pentothal is not working. He doesn't know what to do. She isn't cooperating. Perhaps she has been trained to withstand questioning. Perhaps she has learned to resist the truth serum.

"I need to know more about Project Cassandra, and Damien Veidt, Rachel. Please?"

She shakes her head loosely. It rolls from side to side. She begins to strain against the wrap with more focus.

Stan starts to panic. Snatches up the syringe again. Draws more of the colorless liquid from the vial.

He grasps one of her arms. She struggles a little, but she is still groggy. He holds it still. He can see the dark vein pulsing near the surface. Just beneath the small scab from the first injection, he slides the needle in. Pauses.

"Rachel, please. I need to know what they know about me. I need to know more about Project Cassandra. Please."

He depresses the syringe. Pushes the Sodium Pentothal into her body.

"Buu Stan, I donn know…" Rachel's eyes glaze over. Become glassy. Her head droops to one side. She stares at him. Confused.

"You do know, Rachel. Tell me."

She does not reply. Continues to stare at him, though her eyes now are unfocused.

"Rachel?" He shakes her gently. Taps her face with a couple of gloved fingers. She does not respond. Her mouth is open, slack.

She is not breathing.

CHAPTER 18
SATURDAY

It is 1.06am. Rachel's body is slumped on the toilet. Stan is slumped against the wall opposite.

He cannot stop staring at her.

Her mouth is open. Dried saliva crusts a line from the corner of her mouth to her chin. Her hands and feet remain tied. She looks like a scared child in supplication to a God that will not listen. Her eyes are glassy, unfocused yet somehow she has pinned Stan with them, her face locked in an expression that seems to ask *why*?

The heavy gloves lie discarded next to him. He cradles his head in his hands. Continues to look at Rachel. He needs to work out what to do.

The spy is dead. She didn't tell him anything, but she won't be following him. He has been careful and, provided he removes all of the evidence, then all she is is a dead junkie.

Nevertheless, he cannot shake the dread. Not the hot

rush of panic, but the cold, dark dread deep in the pit of his stomach. Nor can he ignore the sadness. He hasn't felt sadness since he was a child. Looking at Rachel, that feeling returns. Like a dead pet or missing parent. He feels the absence, the deprivation, keenly.

He isn't certain what to do. But, he has to do something. He puts his gloves back on before pushing himself up from the tiles. Picks up his bag.

He walks to Rachel, avoids looking into her eyes. Squatting, he takes the vial of Sodium Pentothal from the metal paper dispenser and puts it in his bag. Unties the Saran Wrap from her arm and stuffs it away. Removes a small pair of nail scissors from the front pocket and saws at the plastic of the cable ties around her feet. By the time the black plastic finally gives his fingers hurt. He flexes his hand before scissoring through the tie around her hands.

As the second cable snaps, Rachel's hands flop to either side. Stan flinches back. Barely avoids falling over. Without life, she is little more than a ragdoll. Despite himself, he is unnerved.

The syringe lies on the floor. Stan picks it up with one gloved hand and guides the needle into one of the two bloody holes in her arm. As he lets it go, the syringe hangs from her arm. The fading elasticity in her skin holds it in place, barely. He watches it oscillate.

There is no paper in any of the cubicles. Stan moves to a sink. Turns on the cold faucet. Water spills out sluggishly. He wets the gardening gloves. The cold, gritty, dirty water dampens the heavy leather.

Back to Rachel. The body. He needs to forget she had a name. She is just meat. He tries to avoid looking in her eyes. Wipes his hands over her face. Rubs the wet leather over her skin. Takes each hand between his and clean them as well.

Finally, he puts her high heels back on her feet. Steps back. Rachel – the body – has sagged down on the metal toilet, her limp fingers almost touching the slightly damp, unpleasant tiles. Her knees are touching, her high-heeled feet spread apart and facing inward. Her head is slumped forward and to one side.

Still, her eyes seem to be staring at him.

He pulls the cubicle door closed. Hides her away from sight. Tries to forget her. Forget what he did.

Stan moves to the heavy metal door and drags it open. Removes the wet gloves and puts them in his bag. Zips it up. Slings it over one shoulder. With a last glance towards the cubicle, Stan heads out.

He sticks to the concrete pathways, avoiding the wider, better-lit paths.

His eyes burn slightly. He wipes them with one hand as he walks, quickly and directly, out of the park.

* * * *

It is 2.08am. Stan has walked west for a little under an hour. The streets are empty except for the occasional taxi or overnight delivery truck. He has moved through expensive residential areas, cheap and dirty streets and various mercantile districts.

He pauses at a trashcan. Unzips his bag and takes all of the Saran Wrap from it. Stuffs the plastic wrap into the can. He is careful not to touch the metal or anything that might be inside. He withdraws his arm, glances around, moves on.

9 minutes later, Stan reaches the waterfront. Piers and docks stretch out into the glistening black water. Waves catch the lights of the city, white and yellow crests.

Without concrete and brick to diffuse it, the wind blowing from the sea is bitterly cold. Stan zips up his jacket, pulls the collar up. It has little effect. The wind cuts through him.

He is shaking as he unslings his bag. Opens it. Withdraws the gloves. Then the cable ties, which he stuffs into the fingers of one glove. Removes the vial from his bag. Places that in the glove. Folds one glove into the other. Flings the glove-ball as far as he can. There is a small splash before it is swallowed.

Stan stares out over the metal railings of the pier. At first he searches for any sign of the gloves, but before long his eyes wander to the skyline. Skyscrapers and apartment buildings, blocks of black, riddled by lights of differing hues.

He turns down his Walkman. Here, on the riverbank, he cannot hear the traffic. There are no people. Just the sound of water lapping against the posts of the pier. And his breath, steaming with each exhalation.

Rachel is dead.

He killed her.

She'll be found in the next few hours. The police will be involved. He's been careful, but they might somehow be able to find him.

And then there's the Tiresias Corporation. They'll be searching for him. Specifically for him. They'll know he killed her.

He doesn't have much time. A matter of days, if he's

lucky.

Shit.

His legs are weak, unable to hold him up. He clutches the railing as he sinks into a squat. He'd thought he was prepared. He'd been preparing for most of his life. But, he is completely unready. Panic clutches his body, wrenches his stomach. He dry heaves, his body shaking so hard he can barely hold on to the metal railings.

Fuck fuck fuck. What does he do? What *can* he do? He needs to control himself. He forces himself to take deep breaths, tells himself he is all right. Everything is OK. He'll be OK. He can do this. He knows what to do.

Slowly, finally, his shuddering subsides. He pulls himself back up. Closes his eyes and steadies himself. Turns the small dial on his Walkman until the endless hiss and crackle fills his mind completely.

Stan needs to take some steps. Clear, obvious steps. He can't keep his flat. He can't keep his storage unit and he needs to escape his job before anyone can find him. Then he needs to find Damien Veidt and kill him. There's no other choice. Rachel is dead and he needs to disappear. But, he can't disappear until he's made sure that Cassandra cannot be created, that those responsible for using it cannot destroy the world. Whether by deliberate action or some mistake, Cassandra will end the world.

Stan breathes in through his nose. Out through his mouth. He avoids closing his eyes. Whenever he does, Rachel's dead, confused eyes stare at him from behind his eyelids. In through the nose, out through the mouth. In through the nose. Out through the mouth.

With a last look over the water, Stan turns and begins his

walk back to the flat. He walks slowly, dazedly, in the darkness. Each time he blinks he is blinded by an epileptic flash. Rachel's face. It takes him sixty-three minutes to reach his apartment.

CHAPTER 19
SATURDAY

He is in his apartment for only a few minutes. He fills his now empty bag with a set of clean clothes. Opens a drawer in the kitchen area and grabs a box of matches. Puts it in the bag as well. Leaves the house.

4.18am. He is in one of the run-down industrial areas of the city. The empty windows of decommissioned factories gape obscenely over sprawling expanses of cracked tarmac. There are few street lights here, fewer still that work. The moon is not quite full and there are few clouds. He can see to walk, and knows this area well.

He walks between the skeletons of buildings, following one of the tarmac roads that used to carry metal, or furniture, or any one of a hundred other things to and from factories and warehouses, before various administrations closed them down, one at a time, or shifted their production lines out of the city or even out of the country. An industrial graveyard. Each dark shell a casualty of progress. A testament to the voracious appetite of humanity. It leaves a bitter taste in his mouth.

Behind an abandoned warehouse are two rows of dirty brick garages, their metal doors uniformly closed. Most look decrepit, the doors ancient, the locks rusted through disuse. As far as he is aware, he is the only person that still uses one. He doesn't pay for it. The company that used to run them went bust years ago.

He checks that no one is around; sometimes kids roam these abandoned places, finding solace in the emptiness and the silence. He is alone. He walks to one of the metal garage doors and squats, pulling out keys as he does. Slides one key into the heavy padlock, twists. The padlock pops open with a click. He lifts the metal door. It rolls up and along the ceiling.

The moonlight does not reach inside. Stan steps in and moves to one side of the doorway. Bends down and picks up the torch he leaves there. Turns it on.

The beam creates a circle of yellow-tinted light, illuminating boxes. Neat stacks of no more than four boxes, organized into three rows, with room to move between them.

The vast majority have Swedish names on them – detergents, washing-up liquid, general cleaning agents. Boxes of mineral water from France and Belgium in the middle row. Toilet rolls from Eastern Europe.

He moves through the first stacks towards the back of the metal unit. Here there are less frequently used goods, including light bulbs and similar.

And, in one corner, a large, red, plastic can of gasoline.

He hefts it in one hand and hauls it to the door. Places

the torch on the ground. Its light shines into the unit, casting his silhouette across the cardboard. He opens a box filled with toilet rolls and removes two. He unravels them and throws the paper over as many boxes as he can. Removes another two rolls and repeats the exercise. Finally, he pulls several rolls apart and builds nests of white paper around the base of the stacks of boxes.

Stan unscrews the cap of the gasoline can and hefts it in both hands. With a swinging motion, he douses the boxes and the toilet paper. Sloshes the liquid as far back as he can, emptying the plastic can. Places it between the stacks of boxes.

He checks again that there is no one around, then takes the clothes out of his bag. He takes off his shirt and sweater, putting on a t-shirt and sweater from the bag. Does the same with his pants and socks. The discarded clothes he stuffs into a box of toilets rolls.

He picks up his torch, turns it off and drops it in his bag. Searches in his bag for the matches. Strikes one. Drops it on the wet toilet paper nest.

Faster than he anticipated, fire roars upwards, devouring the gasoline, paper and cardboard. The heat is immense. He can feel a small explosion is building. Stan quickly backs away from the flames and grabs the metal door. Drags it down to the floor. Quickly walks away.

He is at the end of the row of units when the explosion sunders the night. The ground shudders. Stan crouches and throws up his arms. Turns.

Behind him, the unit is a roaring conflagration. The metal door, buckled and twisted, has been thrown away. Fire thrusts upwards into the pre-dawn sky. Orange light washes out over the units. An ever-growing beacon.

Stan runs. He is back on the tarmac road that leads out of the industrial park when a second explosion rumbles through him. He keeps running until he is back on the street. He pulls the hood of his jacket over his head, and forces himself to walk, not run, away from the area. He does not take any detours on the way to the apartment. The streets are still quiet and mostly deserted. He keeps to residential areas rather than high streets or commercial districts.

He is forcing himself to stay calm. He still sees Rachel's face behind his eyelids. And now, he has set fire to a large portion of his life. He will have to start anew once this is done. Once he's saved the world. If he survives. If he can escape the police, the government. If he can keep afloat, not give in to the fear. He can't act irrationally or succumb to panic. He was never intending to kill anyone, but it is too late for regrets. He has been waging a quiet war for years. Now, his hand has been forced. In war, people must die. Veidt must die.

Underneath his coat he is sweating. The sheer scale of what he intends, the audacity of it, assails him with every step. Every car is searching for him. Distant sirens almost drive him into alleyways to hide.

He cannot possibly succeed.

He cannot fail.

He is home by 5.10am. It is still dark. He does not turn the lights on in the apartment. He has so much to do, but he is exhausted. He has been awake for nearly twenty-four hours. The curtains are still closed from Friday morning. The apartment is dark and peaceful. Stan turns on the stereo, removes his Walkman and falls on to his bed. He is sure that sleep will not come; he closes his eyes and Rachel's face is there. Her eyes, cold and dead, still manage to convey disgust. Her mouth is crusted with her own saliva.

Despite the fear of the nightmares that will surely find him in his sleep, Stan cannot stay awake. He drifts into unconsciousness staring in to Rachel's beautiful eyes and hearing the sounds of fire.

He opens his eyes to fire. Flames surround him. He stands and almost falls again. The ground beneath him wobbles and shifts. He is standing on a small iceberg. White beneath his feet, colorless like glass at the edges as it turns to water in the heat.

Rising above the flames he sees a man, pale faced. He is dressed like a Roman Emperor. Stan recognizes the face. It is always the same face. The face of the man who will start the end of everything.

The Emperor raises his arms and the skies begin to burn. The fires around Stan rise higher and higher. The stars catch light. The iceberg shrinks at an alarming rate.

Suddenly Stan is holding something. Long, wooden. It is comforting in his hands. Without thinking, he raises it and pulls back his arm to throw.

The ice on which he stands is barely large enough to stand on. He struggles to keep his balance as the flames grow closer. Above him, the sky has been swallowed by the Emperor's fires.

The heat has robbed him of his strength. He cannot make the throw.

Rachel's arms reach around him. She kisses his cheek. He turns to her and their lips meet. She breathes into him and he feels her strength join his. He looks in to her eyes. They are beautiful. Pained. Dying.

Her face seems drawn, lifeless. The last of her breath fills his lungs and she dies, still clutching him.

The ice beneath him is like glass. Water pours away from his feet. He steadies himself, hefts the wooden spear and throws.

The spear lurches through the burning air, blackening as it flies. He watches it arc towards the Emperor.

With a crack, the ice beneath him crumbles. Stan is plunged into the water. He cannot see if he killed the Emperor, or if the world burned. Rachel's corpse clings to his legs and he sinks. Deeper, deeper...

Stan lurches awake with a heaving breath. He is still dressed. The room is shadowed in a way that suggests it is daylight beyond his curtains. The radio is still on.

He is gasping, but he tries to breathe deeply. Regain control. He has a headache. A pounding in his skull. He draws in breath slowly through his nose, blows it out through his mouth.

He checks his clock: 2.21pm. He forces himself to walk to the fridge. Pulls out a bottle of water and takes a long swallow.

Toasts the last of his loaf of bread. Bites down on it, but cannot bring himself to eat or swallow. The idea of actually consuming food, of doing something so mundane, makes him nauseous. He has no appetite. Nerves and a strange sense of guilt for Rachel have filled him up already. He chokes down the last of his bottle of water and moves to his computer.

Once he has connected to the World Wide Web, he begins searching. What he is looking for should be harder to find. He starts with obvious ideas – corporate information, conspiracy theorist websites linking CEO's of major corporations to Vietnam, the Falklands conflict and the Cold War. Moves on to searching for specific references of Damien Veidt. There are a number of references to him, all in a professional capacity. His innovative views on technology, his various world-changing ideas and creations.

3.43pm. Stan is still searching. He has trawled through various company announcements and sites discussing the Tiresias Corporation and all its developments.

3.58pm and he rubs his eyes and leans back on his chair. Fetches another bottle of water from the fridge. He contemplates food, but immediately feels sick.

Instead, he gathers some more clothes and stuffs them in his bag. Adds two bottles of water. He has one sharp knife (used for cutting bread), which he also puts into the bag, before returning to his computer.

He continues to browse articles and online forums. Comes across an article of recent advancements online. Including a website that collates all the phone directories in the country. Whitepages. Stan smiles wryly. Of course, after years of Cold Warfare against The Tiresias Corporation and Delphic Electronics, subtly trying to find out about the CEOs, their plans and objectives, now there is a website that simply lists their home addresses for him. It is almost too simple.

He types in Damien Veidt's name. The site spends a few minutes trawling through the accumulated data. Stan waits. The screen flickers in the darkened room, and he is suddenly aware that he hasn't opened the curtains. Not a bad thing given his need to be unnoticed.

Finally, the searching page is replaced by four results.

Damien Veidt	**Portland, OR**
Damien Veidt	**Ossining, NY**
Damien S Veidt	**New York, NY**
Damien K Veidt	**Miami, FL**

Beneath these four are a number of other Veidts and other surnames that the search feels are similar enough to be flagged up.

It is unlikely, although not impossible, that the head of The Tiresias Corporation lives in Miami or Portland. Stan has little way to ascertain either way. So, he is forced to discount them. He clicks on Damien S Veidt, New York, NY.

Less than a minute later and an address in Queens is displayed. Stan hopes that the Veidt he is seeking doesn't live in Queens.

Ossining. Westchester. Westchester, where else would the CEO of a hugely successful, multinational corporation live? Stan clicks on the second Damien Veidt.

Waits.

His heart is beating fast and hard. When he breathes, he can hear he is shaking.

Finally, the address appears:

Damien Veidt
Hillside Villa
Overhill Road
Ossining Village
NY 10562

He stares at it. The address of the man who is currently creating something that will bring about the end of the world. Stan is already certain that he has seen Damien Veidt's face in his dreams. Now he knows where to go. He reads and re-reads the address, committing it to memory.

Stan closes the internet window. Deletes the internet history and data cache. Turns off his computer. He walks to the kitchen, opens a drawer and removes a small screwdriver. Back to the computer.

He unplugs all of the cables and turns the computer around. Unscrews the four small screws holding the cover on and removes it. Inside is a jumble of wires and electrical panels. He pulls out the wires connected to the hard drive, unscrews the metal plates holding it in place. Removes the hard drive. Places it in his bag. Screws the plates back in, replaces the cover and fixes it in place. Puts the computer back in its place and plugs it back in, along with the keyboard, mouse and monitor.

Stan pulls out his clothes boxes from under the bed. Empties them on to the bed. Begins emptying the cardboard boxes of research and newspaper articles as well. Dozens of boxes full of paper clippings, print-outs, scribbled notes. He pours out paper from cereal boxes, pulls out more paper from shoe boxes and turns the larger boxes upside down.

Papers spill from the pile in the middle of the bed, cascading to the floor. Eventually, there are no more boxes to empty. The bed is a mound of paper.

Stan turns back to the kitchen. Opens the fridge and empties every bottle of water in to the sink. Crushes the bottles and slides them under the bed. Puts the pack of cheese in to his bag.

The fridge is emptied, papers and clothes piled up in the

middle of the room. He picks up his bag. Reaches inside for his matches again.

He pauses. Accumulated on the bed before him is his life's work. And, now, ahead of him is its culmination. He is not sentimental, but he finds it hard to let go of this. Without this work, what will he be? If he is successful he will save the world. And have nothing left.

With a shake of his head, he opens the matchbox. His worries are irrelevant. He has spent so long preparing for this final act, this end to the war that, until now, has been waged through espionage. There is no going back. They know he knows. Their spy is dead. Project Cassandra is underway and will, no doubt, be completed soon. Unless there is no driving force. No head to the serpent.

He steels himself for the truth. There is no going back. There never was. Rachel died so that Stan could live, so that Stan could save the world from a war that would destroy everyone.

Stan strikes a match and tucks it in to the pile of clothes and papers. Lights another and tucks that into a different place. Then a third. Twists up a print-out and lights it from a match. Pushes the burning paper into a woolen sweater in the middle of the pile. It catches quickly. Paper and fabrics begin to burn and brown. In moments he is staring at a bonfire.

He throws the matchbox into the blaze. Turns off the stereo and walks out of his apartment. He doesn't bother to lock it. Placing his headphones over his ears, he runs down the stairs and out on to the street. He walks quickly away from the apartment block. Takes the first corner.

Just as he turns, he looks back. Smoke is leaking out

through the gaps in his windows. Before long, the heat will cause the glass to crack and, for the second time, flames will reach towards the sky and consume his life.

He feels empty inside. As if, by burning everything he owns, he is somehow burning himself. His self. He clenches his jaw. This is not a bad thing. There is nothing to tie him to anything anymore. He is anonymous and, as each moment passes, he is becoming... something greater. A hero. A savior.

Two fire trucks swing around the corner, their sirens blaring over the sound of static. As they roar past him, Stan allows himself a tight smile.

CHAPTER 20
SATURDAY

5.51pm. Stan walks past his office one last time. It is risky, but he hopes that the Tiresias Corporation won't have anyone watching the office on the weekend. As he approaches the building, he imagines it shrinking, disappearing. Vanishing from his life. He will not be returning to the swastika-shaped desk. He is not that person anymore. He is greater, more important. He walks past the office, glances at the revolving glass door. Walks on.

His route is twisted, convoluted. At each turn and corner he looks over his shoulder, searching for faces that he has seen before. For the first twenty minutes, Stan is reasonably certain that no one is following him. But, as he turns off one of the busier streets and moves down a quieter avenue, he glances over his shoulder.

There is a man behind him.

Stan hunches his shoulders and keeps walking. Takes the first turning on his right. The road is residential, run down.

He speeds up.

The man turns in to the road. He is a little shorter than Stan. Dark hooded sweater that looks too young for him. He is keeping pace, head down. Street-gazing.

Stan keeps walking. This block is long, straight and quiet. A family passes by noisily across the street. The little girls shouting and singing, their squeals pushing against the wall of white noise. He can see their mother calling them back, the father oblivious to the sounds.

The trees are skinny, stunted. Unable to grow in the choked air of the city. As is so often the case, the houses are set back from the sidewalk, up short flights of steps. There is nowhere to hide. Stan keeps walking as fast as he can without running, or looking obvious. He is scared. How did they find him so quickly? Have they had someone watching the house?

He remembers the car, the slow-moving black sedan, last Saturday. He has been stupid. The resources arrayed against him are overwhelming. He has never had a chance to avoid them.

He cannot hide. So, it's a race. He can only hope that they do not know the extent of his knowledge. If they did, he surely wouldn't be walking. He'd be locked up or dead. So, he has to do what needs to be done. Quickly. Get out of the city, find Veidt, stop him.

For now, he needs to find a way to evade his stalker.

He approaches the next corner. At the last minute, he turns down it, back towards the busy road. He scampers for a few seconds, trying to put more distance between him and his follower. Slows down to his fast walk. Hands in pockets, bag across his shoulders.

He doesn't look back. Doesn't need to. He can feel that he is being followed. He walks hurriedly towards the bustle of people ahead. As he reaches the slow-moving steam of humanity, he glances over his shoulder.

The hooded man is gone.

Stan looks around, left and right, searching for him. He is nowhere to be seen. Stan steps into the human traffic and is swallowed. He weaves his way through the unwashed Saturday shoppers. He is travelling in the right direction, though he had hoped to avoid having to traipse at such a slow pace. And, in a throng of people, it is harder for him to ensure that he isn't being followed, or to spot whoever is tailing him.

He toys with turning down the volume on his Walkman, but decides it is safer to keep his thoughts hidden and focused. Instead, he goes against his instincts and looks about him. Takes in faces, shapes. Tries to mark and remember every feature. Searches for the man in the hooded sweater.

He walks down main streets and busy avenues. If it is hard for him to spot those who might be after him, he hopes it is equally hard for them to pick him out of the crowd. It is a two-hour, straight-line walk from his office to the railway station. Longer than that as he ducks and turns through the twisted grids of the city.

Stan slips between pedestrians, avoiding contact with anyone as best he can. He is acutely aware of his bag, his body, other people. He tries to make himself smaller as he squeezes along the clogged arteries of a bloated city. In the past he would have reflected on how, perhaps, saving these people might not be the best thing for the planet.

But now, after the message Stan read announcing Project Cassandra, the imminence of events makes such thoughts seem crass. False. When death is a distant possibility, it is acceptable to wish it, to invite it on all these people around him. But now it is a looming, all-too-real finality to a series of events. A flood he hopes to divert from all those he had previously condemned.

His mind comes back to the immediate. Once again, he leaves the busy high street and continues North on his way to the station. The streets are cleaner, the houses larger. The stores have a village, boutique feel to them. Bakeries are patisseries, the minimart is organic. There are more families here. Young professionals with their children.

Stan stops to cross. Looks left and right.

Catches something out of the corner of his eye.

Looks left again.

The man in the dark hooded sweater is walking towards him.

Panic.

Stan crosses the road. Walks as quickly as he can. Takes the first turn. As soon as he is out of sight, he runs for a few moments. He runs behind a parked car (red, only two doors, old) and drops to his hands and knees. He has never done anything like this, and such close proximity to filthy asphalt turns his stomach, but he forces himself to remove his bag and then shuffle his body under the car.

His toes push against the road. Fierce stabs of pain shoot through his elbows as he claws his way under the vehicle. Stops. He tries to be still, resting as little of his body on the asphalt as possible. He can feel his knees and elbows gathering soot and dirt.

Footsteps. Quick, quiet thuds on the concrete sidewalk. He sees white-toed sneakers moving swiftly towards him. Slow down. Stop. Stan could reach out and touch one. He holds his breath to avoid making any sound.

The sneakers shuffle one way, then the other. One of them taps impatiently on the sidewalk. Stan is certain the man is waiting for him. He knows. Stan begins inching away. His lungs hurt from holding his breath.

The man's foot stops moving. Stan freezes. Stillness. Just the sound of static in his ears. The sneakers turn away and recede. In seconds, they are out of sight.

Stan stays under the car for several minutes. The sneakers do not return. He does his best to scan around, but he cannot see them. Eventually, he slides himself out on to the road. Stands. Half-heartedly attempts to wipe the blackness from his pants and jacket. He looks around. Then he puts up his hood and moves quickly towards the station.

He tries to focus. He has become something more than this quivering, nervous man who is running scared. He is greater. He is failing to convince himself. He is terrified. An insignificant irritation to a beast so powerful that by rights he should already be dead.

But, he is not dead. He is alive and has just evaded another attempt to stop him. Each step takes him closer to the end. To the world's salvation. And his glory. His vindication. It will all have been justified. His life, Rachel's death. Everything. He just needs to get to Ossining.

By 6.49pm, when he reaches Grand Central Station, he is once again confident. The incident with his follower has dwindled to a footnote. He is too important to be stopped now. Nothing can prevent him from reaching Ossining.

Reaching Veidt. Saving the world.

He walks to a row of windows against one wall. Each window is covered in a thick metal grille. Most have people leaning close to the bars and talking loudly at an attendant on the other side. Stan moves to one that is free.

The woman behind the bars is bored-looking. Middle-aged, droopy-eyed. Her hair is white at the roots and a sickly brown everywhere else. She looks at him expectantly.

"I want to go to Ossining."

She leans forward and taps into a computer.

"One way?"

"Yes." He won't be coming back, at least not to here. He looks around as she types on the computer. She says something about how much it will cost. He hands her money. His thoughts are elsewhere. He cannot see the man with the hooded sweater. He's safe.

She slides the ticket through the slot at the base of the window, along with a couple of bills and some coins. Stan takes the ticket and puts it in a pocket. Leaves the change. He ignores the teller as she calls to him, tapping on the window.

He walks to the large boards hoisted above the ticket offices. Black with white writing. As the fake digital clock ticks and departure times come and go, the boards whirr and clack, replacing departed trains with trains yet to leave the station.

Stan's eyes scan down the list of towns and stations on each departure board. Ossining is on the third board. It is the 21st name listed. The train departs at 19:25. Thirty-one minutes to wait. Thirty-one minutes during which he has to keep safe, unnoticed.

He is painfully aware that his shoes squeak on the shiny marble floor of the station. The station itself is a large, high-vaulted cavern of off-white. Empty of seats, devoid of any furniture or comfort for people who might be waiting.

Stan walks to one of the numerous small corners. A spot where two of the unpleasant walls meet. He squeezes himself in to the space. Leans against one of the corner walls, crosses his arms and waits. Keeps his head down, cap pulled low. His eyes roam the room, searching for the man in the hooded sweater.

Minutes count down. The station is bustling. People pass him by, walking or running. Others wait, sitting on the floor, standing against walls. There are few people in suits, who pace slowly. Even as he watches, more commuters filter in. The station seems to be filling with people. Stan cannot help but think of pens filled with cattle. Or something more malign. People huddled into carriages, crammed into wooden boxes. Starving, frightened. Awaiting death.

He watches a grotesquely obese man lumber to a ticket window and request his tickets in labored gasps. Across the way, a woman in a pinstripe suit drops a waxed cup of coffee. Dark liquid erupts as the cup meets the marble floor. The woman's hands go up. She hops backwards to avoid being scalded. The coffee steams as it spreads across the floor, languidly reaching in all directions. The woman looks up at the departure board. Down at the coffee. Rushes towards a platform. A few minutes later (three minutes and ten seconds), a black man in an orange vest pushes a metal bucket on wheels with a wooden mop to clean up the spill.

At 7.18pm, the boards rotate noisily. The train going to Ossining now has a platform. With a last glance around the station, Stan picks his way through the crowds and towards the train.

CHAPTER 21
SATURDAY

The train rattles out of the station. He can feel the wheels as they shudder over sleepers and joints in the rails.

Stan sits in one corner of the carriage, hidden behind other seats and travelers. He keeps his arms crossed around his bag to avoid touching anything. The seats are dirty, the walls covered in a fine film of sweat, breath and other substances he doesn't want to think about.

At the first stop, the doors slide open and a large number of people get on. No one gets off. The carriage sways slightly. Stan thinks about moving to the middle of the two seats, further away from the walls of the train. As he resolves to move, a small child in a dark blue baseball shirt hops on to the seat next to him. Smiles gormlessly. Turns his back on Stan and gestures excitedly as he talks to the man Stan supposes is the boy's father. Stan looks at the back of the seats in front of him. Unintelligible words are scratched into the hard molded plastic.

The noise of the train as it goes through tunnels between stops threatens to overwhelm his Walkman. He thumbs the volume. So loud it makes him wince.

The carriage is crammed with people. Stan is surprised by this. He had not realized that people would want to travel on a train heading out of the city on a Saturday night. Of course, the train stops at several places in the city before leaving it.

He dimly takes note of a certain uniformity among people on the train. There is something about them that makes them seem more of a pack than he would have anticipated. There are so many, crowded on to seats, standing between them. Dozens crushed into the standing areas, clinging to the wobbly handgrips that oscillate to the rhythm of the train.

The train slows as it pulls into another station. There is a communal shuffling. People crane their necks and shift their feet. Stan cannot read the first sign, nor the second. The train comes to a stop with a slight forward jolt. Out the window, Stan can finally see the station name: Yankees – East 153rd Street.

The doors slide open. The pack spills out of the train, those at the back pushing those in front. Like blue-and-white penguins, the Yankees supporters shuffle and waddle out of the carriage.

The carriage almost empties. Four people are left. Stan studies them. It is painfully clichéd. A thin woman in a suit, a young couple whose lips are locked together and a hobo. Stan snorts to himself. It feels like the beginning of a film.

Or a set-up.

Suddenly, he is on edge. Watches this stereotyped

diorama for any sign of falsity. The woman pulls out a pager device. Are the couple really kissing? He can only see the man's face. His eyes appear to be closed. The woman is squinting at the pager in the poor light afforded by the weak train strip-lights. The hobo appears to be dozing, his chin resting on his chest at an angle Stan feels should be too uncomfortable for sleep.

Stan slowly unzips his bag. Slips one hand inside and grasps the handle of the bread knife. He keeps his hand inside the backpack. Watches.

The woman in the suit tucks her pager away. Crosses her legs and leans back in her seat. She does not look at Stan. The couple stop kissing, but remain in close proximity, touching each other. They whisper and giggle. He can see their gestures, their publically displayed intimate moments. The man strokes her cheek. Stan feels like an unwilling voyeur. Looks away. He feels slightly nauseated, like a boy forced to watch his parents.

The train shudders through eight other stops. Each time, Stan hopes someone will get off, proving his fears unfounded. They don't. A Japanese family of four board the train at one stop. After some frantic discussion and gesticulating, they leave the train at the next station.

It is another ten stops to Ossining. Another twenty-something minutes of perching on his seat, waiting for something to happen. His nerves are already jangling from the imprecision of the train timetable. The times for arriving at each station seem to be more of a guideline than anything else. A minute either way seems acceptable. It is not.

The woman stands. Walks with surprising ease to one of

the sets of doors. She is closer to Stan than she was. He tenses. Ready to use the knife if he has to. Four on one, he doesn't have much of a chance, but he cannot let them stop him.

The train slows. The couple also stands. She has one arm around his waist, he has one around her shoulders. He reaches up, his free arm moving from one train handle to another. She leans on him for support.

He glances at Stan. Whispers something the girl's ear. She looks at Stan, smiles. It is not a friendly smile. A mocking smile. Despite himself, Stan whimpers. All three stand together, facing a set of doors. The young man glances towards Stan again. Looks away.

The train pulls in to a station and stops. The doors open. The suited woman steps off. The young woman follows, tugging the young man by the hand. He casts a final look in Stan's direction before leaving the train.

Stan sighs with relief. Only the tramp remains on the train. Still appears unconscious.

The doors begin to close. A middle-aged man in a casual shirt, jacket and pale blue jeans slides between them. He looks in Stan's direction. Looks the other way. Walks towards Stan's end of the carriage. Takes a seat halfway between the doors and where Stan sits. Pulls a book from inside his jacket and begins to read.

The hobo snores himself awake at Tarrytown and lurches out of the train, arms wind-milling, muttering to himself. Clearly crazy. Stan feels his lip curl in derision. The strange thing about cities is that they can be too much. Something about the closeness, the speed and the noise. It can bend and break and warp a mind.

Finally, at 8.13pm, the train pulls in to Ossining. Stan gets to his feet. He clutches his bag to his chest, one sweaty hand still inside and holding the dry wooden handle. The man continues to read. Does not seem to even look in Stan's direction.

The doors open and Stan steps out on to the train platform. A few other people leave other train cars. They all head in the same direction. Away from Stan. Stan waits. The man in the carriage is still reading. The doors slide shut and, with a slight judder, the train moves off. He is left alone on the platform.

He zips up his bag. Slings it over his back. Wraps his jacket tightly around him to try and ward off the unseasonably cool evening.

The platform back into the city is busier. Young adults and teenagers littering the night, waiting to head to Tarrytown or even up into the city itself to get drunk, dance and kiss. Living their faintly sordid lives (or as sordid as one can get while living in million dollar homes), ignorant to the fact that, without him, they will almost certainly never live to regret their indiscretions, to try to teach their children not to make the mistakes they made, to watch their children make them anyway. They will know only fire and fear and death.

Up the metal-plated steps. The ticket office is empty. Clean and white, but devoid of life. Faint smell of cleaning agents. To one side of the ticket office window is a plastic rack. Train timetables and maps of Ossining. Stan takes a map. Steps out on to the concrete sidewalks of Ossining.

CHAPTER 22
SATURDAY

Ossining is lit with a phosphor-white glow. There is little in the way of Saturday night traffic as Stan walks down the ramp from the station to the town. The air is cold, made colder by the breeze from the Hudson River at his back. Before him, a small square of stores – a deli, a post office. It is almost offensively affluent and small-town.

Behind the obvious village feel, however, are the signs of a commuter haven for those who want to live out of the city, but have its comforts. An up-market Chinese restaurant two stores down from a faux-Mexican diner.

Stan follows the main street for a few minutes. It is quiet. A few people are out, couples heading to supper or to see a movie. A few teenagers who are too young to head out of Ossining to somewhere else. They loiter on the streets, finding spots where a few can sit together. They laugh and chat. Stan crosses the road to avoid them. Their casual jubilance unsettles him.

He reaches a crossroads. Finds a street light and unfurls his map. He spends a short while reviewing the map. Finds Overhill Road and works out his route. Folds up the map, turns left and keeps walking.

The road ascends before him. A gradual but insistent hill. Stan watches the ground as he walks. Keeps his route at the forefront of his mind. Away from the city, the sidewalks are cleaner, somehow older but fresher. Less traffic, perhaps even something of a consideration for the streets on which people live.

The night has become overcast. Clouds sit heavily above the town. The wind pulls and tugs at him. He keeps his hands deep in his pockets, his shoulders hunched and head down. Walks. The road ends in another crossroad. He turns right. Overhill Road.

This road is wide. A ruler-straight tree-lined avenue. Cars in driveways, large houses set back from the sidewalk. Lawns glisten. There are even white picket fences. Suburban castles.

Stan's insides are churning, roiling beneath the skin. He is so close now. Soon he will be staring at the house of the man whose plans will destroy the world. A man who must be stopped, because he will not choose to stop. The mastermind behind Project Cassandra. Damien Veidt.

He has been walking along Overhill Road for eight minutes before he realizes that he is looking for a name on one of these distant buildings. In the night he can barely see front doors, let alone any names. He swallows his frustration. He has made it this far, he will find the right house.

A further three minutes and he is walking past walled complexes and mansions with high fences and electric entry gates. The sort of home the CEO of a global, government-subsidized technology company might well own. Stan slows. Examines the plaque on the brick pillar of the first mansion's wall.

Thistledown

Stan isn't sure he even knows what that is, or what it might mean. It is irrelevant. He moves to the next plaque on this side of the street. It feels like it takes minutes to walk from one mansion to the next.

He crosses the road and checks the mailbox affixed to the intricate wrought iron gates of **1267 OVERHILL ROAD**. Spends another minute walking to the next house. Crosses back over. Occasionally goes back on himself to ensure that he has not missed any.

He is shaking with cold and nerves. He has been checking house names for 19 minutes. He is starting to panic. Perhaps he got the street wrong, or the name, or even the wrong town. His legs are shaking uncontrollably, as if he is about to vomit, or just has. As if he is barely in control of his body.

He can't have got it wrong. If he has, he's fucked. The world is fucked. He must have got the right Veidt, the right address. He doesn't make mistakes like that. He realizes he is whispering to himself. "It must be here. It must be here."

He checks another house. This one has solid wooden gates, with the words *The Fitzpatrick Residence* carved in to it in pretentious lettering.

Stan crosses the road again. He has not seen a car or passerby since he started walking up the hill. Perhaps those that were going to go out are already out, the remainder staying in. This house's metal gate has a mailbox affixed to one side. The writing on it is small, sensible. He has to get close to it to make it out. His breath catches. Stomach lurches. His tongue is suddenly too large for his mouth.

HILLSIDE VILLA

He stares at the bronze writing. It is carved into the metal of the mailbox. He tries to imagine what the lettering could mean. What it might say about the occupier. Fails. It does not scream harbinger of the apocalypse. It doesn't suggest a man so obsessed with his creations that he will pursue a course of action regardless of the consequences. It is, if anything, dull. Boring. Safe.

It is 9.45pm. In all likelihood, Veidt is home with his family. He must have children, they all have children. Probably a girl and a boy. And Stan cannot kill Veidt in front of them.

Perhaps he can sneak in to the house while they sleep. The thought unsettles him. He won't be able to sneak in to a gated complex at night. What if they have a dog? What if he doesn't find the right room? He could wake someone. It would be over. He, and the world, will have lost.

He stands before Hillside Villa and tries to think of other options. Nothing comes to mind, other than waiting for an opportune moment. Perhaps they will order food to be delivered. Failing that, Stan might get a chance in the morning. For now, he is going to have to wait.

There are a few cars parked on the street. Trees every sixty paces or so. Stan dimly remembers he passed a bench not long ago, but is unsure if it has a clear view of Veidt's house. He retraces his steps until he finds the bench. It is not far from Hillside Villa. The gates are visible even in the dark. He is worried that he is too far away, but he cannot simply stand there, waiting, for hours.

The bench is old, weathered. Wooden slats and metal rivets. There is a small plate screwed into one of the slats on the bench's back. A memorial. Stan doesn't read it. Sits. The wood warms quickly beneath him. It is 9.52pm.

He stares at the gates for some time. His mind is empty. Or, rather, it is filled only with the gates, what they mean, his future. He feels tensed, poised. For some unknown reason, he expects the gates to open for him. He cannot not look. If he looks away, he'll miss the instant when the electricity hums and the gates judder in to life.

They remain inert. Lifeless. Uncooperative. Stan sighs and turns the volume on his Walkman down. It is quiet here. He doesn't need the white noise to be loud. He leans back on the bench. It is going to be a long night.

At 10.30pm, the twin beams of car headlights make their way along Overhill Road. The car is moving quickly. Stan cannot help but hope that the car is destined for Hillside Villa. A ridiculous cosmic contrivance. The car does not slow. Stan lowers his head, hiding his face in the shadow of his cap. The car passes. He watches the red taillights diminish. All that is left is static.

He turns back to the gates. Waits. Arms crossed. After a while, his neck hurts. The cold is seeping in to his hands and feet. He stands, paces around the bench. Back and forth over the unmarked concrete. To let the time pass he lets his mind wander. Rachel lurches, unbidden, into his mind. Her corpse. Her dead, empty, pleading eyes. Filled with betrayal. He shakes his head, once. It was not betrayal, but the shock of being caught. He believes this. Has to believe this. A wave of nausea. Swallows hard. Snatches a bottle of water from his bag and drinks deeply.

Keeps pacing. The sickness passes, though his stomach clenches should he let his thoughts wander back to that bathroom in the park.

11.04pm. The wind has picked up. Stan is huddled on the bench. He has put on his extra clothes. He doesn't feel the chill so much through the layers. The gate remains closed and unmoving. He has watched the comforting lights of various homes die with the touch of a button. The full moon is hidden by the fat, violent clouds. As the houses grow dark, the world seems to shrink around him. As if the light held back the claustrophobic truth of the world. It is not a vast open place, but a tiny, smothering thing.

He rises. Walks to the middle of the road, as far from the walls and trees and the uncomfortable closeness of shadow as possible. Walks along one of the two yellow lines. Follows it to Hillside Villa.

Beyond the gates, the house is dark. Curtains are drawn. Without light, the building seems dead. Inside, the family sleeps. Stan wonders if Veidt manages to sleep at night, or if the horrible, inescapable truth of the evil he will perpetrate against the world leaves him lying in his bed, staring at the ceiling. He doubts it. More likely, he sleeps like a child, deep and untroubled.

Regardless, the gates are closed and locked. They are ten

feet high, each metal railing spear-shaped. The bars are set far enough apart that he could place his feet between them, but the thought of trying scares him. The thought of being trapped on the wrong side petrifies him.

Frustrated, he walks back to the bench. Sits. Drinks. Waits. He continues to watch the gate expectantly. Brings his feet up on to the bench and leans his side against the wooden slats. Blinks. Shakes his head. Blinks again.

CHAPTER 23
SUNDAY

The gates swing open silently. He walks between them. Feels watched. The door to the house is heavy, black-painted wood. The knocker is a large, brass ring. Stan takes it in one hand. Knocks once, twice. The sound is strange. It sounds like a death rattle. Like the last breath of a dying woman. It echoes around the building. He steps through the door.

Inside. He walks through a few inches of frigid water. Syringes float around his ankles. He steps carefully to avoid them. Needles glint in the sourceless light. He looks ahead. The corridor extends endlessly before him. He looks to either side, seeking a door. There are none.

The familiar man walks down the corridor toward him. The face that Stan has come to associate with Damien Veidt. Behind him lurks death. It hides in his shadows, a monster made of bullets, with grenades for eyes. Missile-claws. Each movement is a quiet rustle and squeak. Stan reaches for his Walkman to turn up the static.

The Walkman is not there. Frantically he runs his hands over his body. No Walkman. No backpack. No weapon.

The man continues to walk slowly towards him. He is talking but making no noise. Stan cannot hear him, does not want to hear him. Death swarms behind him, filling the hall. Obscuring the light.

The familiar man smiles warmly. Extends his hand. It is a welcoming gesture. Stan tries to back away, but the door is closed behind him. He is trapped. The man's words are an inviting sibilance. They fill his ears, hissing and whispering promises he cannot understand. Stan shakes his head frantically, tries to scream to drown out the man's words. But, he can make no sound. He screams again. Silence.

The water rises. It is up to his knees. His waist. The man floats calmly above the rising water, his hand extended. Stan need only take it and he will be safe. The water is up to his chest. Bullets swirl around him, needles prick his skin. Stan's own blood mingles with the dark water.

Stan screams again. Empties his lungs of air. Tries to draw breath. Water spills in. Bullets fill his mouth. He will drown. Water splashes in his eyes. And above stands the man who will destroy the world. He is still smiling.

Stan sinks beneath the water...

A fat drop of rain bursts on Stan's face. Another. Within moments, sheets of water lash down on him. He scurries to the nearest tree. The late spring blossom offers some shelter from the rain. Stan clutches his bag to his chest and watches the rain. Within minutes, the gutters are flooded, streams of rainwater tumbling along the road. Puddles reflect the cold, violent glow of the streetlights. The mirror-sheen ripples under the rain's assault.

He checks his watch. 4.26am. Somehow, he has slept away a good portion of the night. Fortunately, it is unlikely that anyone has come or gone from Hillside Villa in the small hours of the night. It is still a case of waiting. The rain's susurration slips between the buzz of his headphones. Despite the persistent gnawing in his stomach, the two entwined noises comfort him. He takes a deep breath. Stares at the gates through the rain. Lets his focus shift. Watches the drops slice through the night. They fall straight down, cutting the world into ribbons. Lines of silver in the dark, tiny meteors trailing white fire in the light of the street lamps. It is nothing more than falling water but, for some reason he cannot entirely understand, there is a sublime intricacy. A simple beauty.

He watches the rain fall. For the first time in a long time, he isn't sure for how long. In a way, being forced to wait has freed him from worrying about time. His eyes move between the rain and the night. The blurry image of gates and walls behind the storm. Something about it all seems wrong. Fake. Like an out-of-focus photograph. A failed attempt to capture reality.

Eventually, the torrent lessens. As the minutes pass, the heavy, black clouds drift away, replaced by a scattering of grey. The downpour is now a light shower. Raindrops lazily pepper the sidewalks. It is growing a little lighter. Somewhere behind him the sun is starting to rise. He checks his watch. 5.52am.

He steps out from under the tree. As he moves, he is aware both of how wet he is and how cold. The tree provided shelter, but enough water got through that his cap is sodden. The rest of him is wet, the wetness chilling his skin. As he gets nearer to the ephemeral moment of action, he grows colder deep inside. The combination leaves him shivering.

He walks to Hillside Villa. The gates are still closed. The lights are off, curtains drawn. Outside, on the street, there are signs that the world is waking up. Stan glances to one side and sees a car moving along the road. He starts walking, slow and calm. The car passes, a tired man in a white shirt and red tie at the wheel. He doesn't look at Stan.

Once the car is out of sight, Stan moves back to the bench. It is water-logged. He walks to the tree once again. The ground is wet, but bearably so. He unzips his backpack, removes the bottles of water and places them on the ground. Takes out the knife and holds it in one hand. Places the backpack on the ground. Sits on it. Puts the knife behind him.

Waits.

Watches the unmoving gates.

Waits.

These quiet hours before waking feel interminable. Stan watches the sky lightening. Birdsong begins to pierce the white noise. He turns up the volume, drowns out the shrill, annoying whistles. At 6.42am, a boy cycles along the road from the direction Stan walked. Stan doesn't move. Sits in the shadows of the tree.

The boy stops, hops off his bicycle and fishes a newspaper from his large, waterproof bag. The first building has a mailbox. He pushes the newspaper into it. Jogs across the street to the house opposite and throws another newspaper through the railings. Back to his bike, cycles on.

He stops again at Hillside Villa. Pulls out a pale orange newspaper and stuffs it into the mailbox slot. Cycles on. He does not notice Stan.

Stan watches the delivery boy stop-start cycling his way along Overhill Road. Stan stands and paces around the tree. The light grey clouds scud away, leaving anemic blue sky, tainted a pale yellow by the slowly rising sun.

Returns to the tree. Sits on the backpack. He wants to close his eyes, but knows that to do so would be foolish. Anyone could see him, accost him. Instead he moves the backpack slightly, adjusts his position so he can clearly see the gates without turning his head. Leans his head against the deeply grooved bark. Moves until he is comfortable. Fixes his eyes on the orange newspaper poking in a vaguely obscene way from the mailbox.

Each time he feels his consciousness slipping, he reminds himself of the enormity of his task. He has to save the world by choosing to kill someone who otherwise will not be stopped. Stan must consciously take another man's life. Something that, in abstract, is seemingly trivial. But, when faced with the power and need to deprive another of life, Stan feels that there is a subconscious block. Some sort of mental wall that screams that to kill is to break one of society's unbidden taboos. Stan smiles at himself. He is imposing such a taboo. Humans have killed each other since they first competed for survival. This is no different. He must kill a man for survival. His and that of all other humans.

More time passes. Stan begins to lose hope. As more cars pass along the road, he gathers up the bottles and knife and place them back in the backpack. Tries to stay out of sight behind the tree as much as possible. He is tired, still wet, terrified he won't get a chance to do what he is dreading having to do.

8.02am. Stan is staring at the gates of Hillside Villa, thinking about Rachel. By now she will have been found. The police will be involved. Rachel's cold, white body will already be on a sterilized metal slab in the basement of a hospital.

The black metal gates of Hillside Villa shudder. Begin to swing inwards. A large, metallic red SUV slips out on to the road. Turns towards Stan. A woman is driving. Petite, auburn hair. A small, excited boy is in the front seat. He is wearing some sort of sports shirt. A smaller, bespectacled girl with hair the same color as her mother's, sits sullenly in the back.

The car swoops past and Stan leaves the shade of the tree and darts across the street. The Black gates are swinging closed. Stan runs, heedless of anyone who might see him. This is his chance. He turns sideways as he reaches the gate. Squeezes between the railings.

He is inside Hillside Villa's walls. Behind him, the gates shut with a solid clang that echoes over the static in his ears.

CHAPTER 24
SUNDAY

Hillside Villa is large and traditionally built. The door is heavy, black-painted wood. The knocker is a brass ring. The similarity to his dream is reassuring. He stares at the door. A shape moves across one of the windows. Veidt must be home.

Stan's heart rises into his throat. He unslings his backpack. Reaches inside and grasps the knife. His hands feel hot and clammy. His breathing is uneven, shuddering. He holds the backpack at his side, one hand holding the knife and part of the bag.

He closes his eyes. Rachel's face flashes before his eyes. He has come too far to turn back. He forces her away. Tries to find a way to calm his breathing. Takes a long, slow breath. Another. His heart has slowed slightly. He opens his eyes. He reaches in to his pocket and turns the volume down on his Walkman. Steps forward and knocks on the door with the brass knocker. One second later, knocks again.

Seconds pass. Stan almost steps back, but refrains. Waits close to the door.

There is a clunk and the door swings inwards.

A man stands in a cream colored hall. He is wearing ridiculous purple and white striped pajamas and a flannel dressing gown. Brown slippers. Stan's eyes quickly move to the man's face. It is pale, his dark hair sticking out from sleep. His eyes, too, are dark. They glare at Stan with suspicion.

It is him. The man from his dreams.

"Can I help you?" His voice is cultured, but still rough from sleep. He has not been awake for long.

Stan works his jaw. Tries to find words. But, faced with his nemesis, he can't find the ability to speak.

The man starts to close the door, reducing the open space between them.

"No!" Stan tries to speak, but produces only a croak. A sandpaper whisper.

"I think you've got the wrong address, Stanny." The man starts to close the door.

Stanny? Perhaps he misheard over the white noise. Perhaps the wet and the tiredness are affecting him. Stan swallows hard, wetting his throat. "What?"

"You have the wrong address, sorry."

"No. You're Damien Veidt."

Less than a foot of space remains. The man's face is all that is visible. The rest is black wood. The man's eyes narrow.

"Yes, I'm Damien Veidt. Are you a reporter or something? I've no comment to make."

"What... What about PC?"

One eyebrow raises. A despot's tell. A failed poker face.

"I have no comment to make about any PC, whatever you might have heard. Goodbye."

The face eases back. The door starts to close. The warm light of the hallway diminishes.

Stan pushes against the door. The wood is strangely warm. Veidt is pushing against him. Stan feels panic rising. And a strange, distant sort of elation.

He throws his shoulder against the door. It slams against the hallway wall. Veidt is thrown to the floor. Stan staggers inside.

Veidt's eyes are wide. Staring. Fearful. Stan follows his gaze. In breaking in, he dropped his bag. The knife is still clutched tightly in one sweaty fist.

Damien Veidt starts to crab-walk backwards, down the hallway. Stan follows. The elation has replaced the fear, the hollow dread. Watching the man who would destroy the world scrabbling on all fours to escape him makes him feel strong, powerful. Right.

Veidt rolls over and finds his feet. Runs the last few feet of the hall and into a living room. The sofa is too sumptuous, striped in silver and white. Stan walks calmly in to the room. It matches the sofa. Too frilly, too ostentatious.

Veidt stands on the other side of the sofa. He is breathing heavily, but he has regained his composure.

Stan begins to walk around the sofa. Veidt moves to keep it between them.

"Who are you? What do you want?" He asks. Stan hears his words dimly, the static in his ears muffling sound.

Making him feel that he is separate from the world. Safe.

"I have to stop you."

"Why? What have I done?"

"PC. Project Cassandra. I can't let you finish it. Can't let you... kill everyone."

"PC? Project Cassandra? What do you mean?"

Stan doesn't reply. He is smiling. He will not be fooled or distracted. He has beaten them all — The Tiresias Corporation, The Government. Veidt. He is more than them. Better than them. He is beyond them all. He is greater. Static fills his head. His fingers flex on the knife handle.

They have reversed places around the sofa. Veidt dashes back out of the living room and turns left. Stan chases. In to the kitchen.

Black and white tiles cover the floor. The surfaces are wood and chrome. An odd fusion of traditional and modern.

Veidt reaches for the heavy wooden knife block on the counter. His hand stretches out for a blade.

Stan grabs Veidt's dressing gown and heaves him backwards.

Veidt shrieks. "No, please! Please! What are you doing?"

Stan tries to force his enemy to the floor. Veidt resists, wriggling and pushing. Gasping and shouting, "No, No!"

But, Stan is more powerful. Stan is right. He is the world's savior. His slips one arm around Veidt's neck. Stands behind him and squeezes.

Drives the knife into Damien Veidt's back. Pushes until his knuckles feel the warm, springy toweling of the dressing-gown. Wetness spills over his hand. The CEO of the Tiresias Corporation jerks and struggles. But, his strength is no match for Stan. Not now. He has shed the chains of his existence, evolved beyond the constraints of his pathetic life. He is greater.

He twists the bread knife. Veidt jerks again, more feebly than before.

Stan's mouth is close to one of Veidt's ears. He leans close and whispers. "I've stopped you. No war. No death. No PC. No Project Cassandra."

Veidt's struggles have all but ceased. His breath bubbles. Blood foams at the corners of his mouth.

Stan lowers him to the tiled floor. Red spills out over the black and white. Veidt is on his side. He coughs. Drags in one wet breath. Exhales.

"Project... ilecalibration."

The gurgling sound stops. Stan kneels on one side. Leans over to look into the face of the man who he has just killed. Damien Veidt's eyes are half-open. Mouth slack. Stan watches a thin line of dark, viscous blood slowly drip to a white tile.

Stan slumps back on to his heels. Sighs. He has done it. He has saved the world. Yet, somehow, he feels unfulfilled. There is something anti-climactic about it. No one calls his name, reaches out to touch him. No one adores him. He has saved them all, and no one knows. No one has witnessed his heroism.

He stares at the small pool under Veidt's body. The dressing down is turning a brownish red, soaking up the spilt blood. Stan sighs again. So be it. Unwitnessed. Unrecognized. But, a hero regardless. He is the world's savior.

He pulls out the bread knife. Clutches it in one, blood-encrusted hand (he never knew it dried so quickly) and heads back to the front door. It is still open. His bag lies on the welcome mat. He picks it up. Drops the knife inside. His sweater is stained. He removes it. The one underneath is drier and unsoiled. He places the dirty sweater in his bag and zips it up. Washes his hands in the kitchen sink. Uses only water. Not the soap. It is purely out of habit. No one will search for him now. He's won.

He smiles. When the authorities investigate, they will discover the truth, They will learn about Project Cassandra. Its applications. Its destructive potential akin to that of the Atomic Bomb. And, they will learn that he was right all along. Perhaps they will search for him. For the man who saved the world. They will call for him, clamor for him. They will realize that he is greater.

He frowns suddenly. A dark thought.

How will he prove to the world that it was him? He recalls his dreams. *He holds something in his hands. A sphere. Uneven and warm.* A trophy. Proof.

He returns to the kitchen. Withdraws the bread knife again. Kneels behind the body. Places one hand on Damien Veidt's head. Begins sawing.

8.13am. Stan opens a kitchen drawer. Pulls out a roll of garbage bags and tears one off. Struggles to open it. Finally manages. Picks up his trophy by the tousled hair. Places it in the garbage bag. Wraps it up as best he can. Places it in his backpack with the bread knife. Zips the backpack closed and slings it over one shoulder.

Stan returns to the front door. Steps outside. Breathes deeply. The air smells sweeter. It lacks the ominous taint to which he has become so accustomed. It is safe. He has done it. Rachel's death was not in vain. The world will not end in chaos and riots. The sound of war will not be the last sound humanity hears. Thanks to him.

Reaching into his pocket, Stan presses the stop button on his Walkman. The familiar sound of static abruptly stops. Silence. He hears a car somewhere. The quiet sound of birdsong. Peaceful noises. He removes his headphones. He has no need of them now. He is safe. He has won.

He closes the heavy door behind him and walks to the gate. Presses the little button. It makes a buzzing sound. Steps back and waits for the gates to open. He cannot stop grinning. He could almost skip.

The pale orange newspaper is still in the mailbox. As the gate finishes swinging open, stopping with a shudder, the paper falls to the ground. Unfurls. It is a business and finance daily newspaper. Stan looks at the headline.

DELPHIC ELECTRONICS ANNOUNCES PROJECT CASSANDRA

The silence is deafening. Stan's eyes hurt from staring at the writing on the paper. His throat is dry. His face is burning, the rest of him freezing. His stomach clenches. If he had anything in his stomach, he'd vomit. His legs are weak and will not support him. His bag feels as if it is squirming on his back.

The sound of a car gets louder. Closer.

Sweating, shaking, Stan looks up at the road.

A black sedan glides in to view with a low growl. He has seen it before. A week ago. It drives past Hillside Villa slowly.

The driver wears a black suit. Black driving gloves. Dark glasses. He turns his head in Stan's direction as the car passes.

Time crawls. Stan stares at the dark glasses. The dark glasses stare at Stan. The message could not be clearer. *We know you. You are watched.*

Stan shakes uncontrollably. Tries to reach into his pocket at the same time as putting on his headphones. The inescapable truth has left him weak, dizzy. He feels as if the air has been punched out of him. Terror, stifling and bone-crushingly heavy, threatens to drive him to his knees.

Standing in the driveway of Hillside Villa, the home of Damien Veidt, the CEO of The Tiresias Corporation and the man Stan had known would try to end the world since he could remember knowing anything, Stan mutters to himself, over and over:

"I got the wrong one. I got the wrong one."

ABOUT THE AUTHOR

Justin Carroll graduated with a degree in English Literature and Language from King's College, London in 2004. In between writing and marketing, he fritters away his time doing all sorts of geeky things. Shortlisted for several short story competitions, Justin was a finalist in the 2010 British Fantasy Awards. *Everything's Cool* is his first published novella.

Printed in Great Britain
by Amazon.co.uk, Ltd.,
Marston Gate.